Other Novels by Mildred Walker
Available in Bison Books Editions

THE
BODY
OF A
YOUNG
MAN
By **Mildred**

Walker

Introduction to the
Bison Books Edition
by Sharon Bryan

University of Nebraska Press
Lincoln and London

⊗ The paper in this book meets the minimum requirements of
American National Standard for Information Sciences—Perma-
nence of Paper for Printed Library Materials, ANSI Z39.48-1984.

First Bison Books printing: 1997
Most recent printing indicated by the last digit below:
10   9   8   7   6   5   4   3   2   1

Library of Congress Cataloging-in-Publication Data
Walker, Mildred, 1905–
The body of a young man / by Mildred Walker; introduction to the
Bison Books edition by Sharon Bryan.
p.   cm.
ISBN 0-8032-9787-4 (alk. paper)
I. Title.
PS3545.A524B65   1997
813′.52—dc21
96-39358   CIP

Reprinted from the original 1960 edition by Harcourt, Brace and
Company, New York.

For F R S

Introduction

Sharon Bryan

Mildred Walker's eleventh novel, which was nominated for a National Book Award when it was first published in 1960, is a beautifully wrought meditation on the meaning, limits, demands, and failures of friendship—especially on what happens when a long-standing relationship is tested and found wanting. The book displays quiet fictional virtues that are old-fashioned in the best sense: it is grounded in complex characters, and the relations among them are as meticulously designed and set in motion as the workings of a Swiss watch. At the same time, it ponders the question of what it means to be a man, and its answer to that is thoroughly contemporary.

On the surface, the story couldn't be simpler: one couple, Phyllis and James, drive from their home in the Midwest to spend the summer in New England with James's old friends, Josh and Lucy. Most of what follows consists of dialogue between and among various combinations of these four main characters. Reviews of the first edition mention Hemingway, and Walker's use of dialogue is in some ways reminiscent of his best work, the early novels and short stories. She is as deft as he was at contrasting the polite small talk of what the characters say with the complexity and intensity of the thoughts and feelings that lie below their words. Much of the pleasure here comes from reading between the lines. The novel is propelled not by dramatic events but by the subtler internal shifts that more often shape our lives.

Although the circumstances at first seem idyllic, we soon learn that the summer reunion was prompted by a phone call Phyllis made to Josh asking for his help. It turns out that the most obviously dramatic event in the book has already taken place offstage: James is a high school teacher, and he has been depressed and guilt-ridden since one of his best students committed suicide several months earlier. Phyllis hopes that Josh will somehow be able to pull James out of his despair. The book's title and epigraph point simultaneously to the boy's suicide and to one of the book's central themes: that friendships must change and grow if they are to survive in the present. The epigraph, a quotation from Virginia Woolf, compares a past friendship to a corpse "laid up in peat for a century," still vivid, "with the red fresh on his lips," but a dead thing nonetheless.

There is always danger in bringing the past up against the present, pitting the burnished memory against the imperfect reality. It is most dangerous of all to do this with old friends. No matter how well we know another person, to a certain extent we invent our friends out of our own needs and wants. Friendship is based on perceived similarities and shared values, and we focus on those to sustain the friendship. As long as the friendship exists in memory or at a distance, as long as no crisis tests it, it can continue as a mutually satisfying abstraction. But sometimes we discover, when past and present are brought together, an unbridgeable gap between the invented character and the actual person.

The friendship between James and Josh is long-standing and powerful, based on respect and affection. But the summer reunion reveals great differences between the two men—differences that have surely been there all along, but have never loomed so large. At first it seems that Josh is confident, self-assured, strong, and reasonable (that is, presumably, why Phyllis turns to him for help) while James is unsure, tentative, given to brooding. As events unfold, however, Josh's belief in the power of will to overcome any obstacle—including emotions—is revealed as rigidity rather than strength. As far as he's concerned, James simply needs to put the boy's suicide behind him and get on with his life. Dwelling on it (i.e., speaking of it at all) will only prolong James's inertia. Soon after James and Phyllis arrive, Josh assures her, "Now that he's here he'll forget all about it." A little later he admonishes Lucy: "We don't want to suggest that the thing is that serious" (serious enough to warrant seeing a psychiatrist). At one point he complains to James, "You're not making any effort to set it aside and go on." But as James complains later, Josh feels that "everything can be handled by sheer willing to do it." Josh's approach to life is classic stiff-upper-lip, rock-ribbed, as unyielding as New England granite. Feelings are to be subdued or overcome by reason and will. Though Josh never uses the word, he clearly considers it "unmanly" to explore or discuss them.

For Josh, the world is black-and-white; for James, it is shades of gray. James has what Keats called "negative capability"— the capacity to live with uncertainty and ambiguity. This openness leaves him more vulnerable to his own emotions—in this case depression—but it also gives him the strength of flexibility, which contrasts sharply with Josh's rigidity-posing-as-strength. What's at issue between the two is no less than what it means to be a man.

In the book's most emblematic scene (not shown, but related after the fact), James and Josh go on a hike they've taken many times in the past, up a nearby mountain. They argue and part ways, and there's some minor suspense about James's whereabouts when Josh returns alone. But James has simply taken a different route down. As he later tells Josh, when Josh says he can see the whole mountain from where he's standing: "Sure you can, both sides of it, the side you came down and the one I came down." This is what Josh is blind to, that there's more than one path. James tells Phyllis: "Josh sees his world in one way and he's not going to admit to other ways of seeing."

It's obvious that James is far more open to change than Josh is—indeed, has sought it out by moving away and by marrying Phyllis. Phyllis is the most interesting of the four main characters—in part because she's the point-of-view character, so we get details of her thoughts, memories, and feelings. One question that arises, as the differences emerge between her vision and Josh's vision of James, is why she turned to Josh for help in the first place. Part of the answer is that she knew Josh only secondhand, knew only the idealized version James had created. But a more important factor is Phyllis's deep insecurity, as we learn in a series of flashbacks to her childhood.

It would be too melodramatic to say that Josh and Phyllis are contesting for James's soul, and would make James a more passive figure than he is. But their contrasting approaches to dealing with emotions represent the extremes James navigates between as he confronts his own guilt and self-doubt. Phyllis wants him to recover from his depression; Josh simply wants

James to put the episode behind him, recovered or not. Walker reveals the differences between the two by having Phyllis gradually revise her sense of what James needs to do to recover.

A friendship between two people is delicately balanced; add one or two more people, and all the weight is redistributed. As Josh says, "After a man's married, you begin to see him fully as another man—the wife he picks changes your idea of him." The two wives reflect and affirm their husbands' differing worldviews. Lucy focuses on maintaining a smooth surface and the status quo, while Phyllis is more open to new ways of looking at things.

These characters are polite and mannerly to the end (it's impossible not to think of Jane Austen), but it's clear that the friendship between James and Josh will never be the same. The summer may not have been quite what any of the four expected, but there's every sense that James and Phyllis are departing both lightened and enlightened. They seem to have been strengthened by what they've learned about themselves, while Lucy and Josh are shaken and unnerved—though they likely will never say so.

The Body of a Young Man borrows many of its techniques from poetry: the compression, the layered imagery, the flair for illuminating metaphor ("Long after they had said good night, Phyllis felt their wakefulness in the dark, the way you could feel a moth in the dark, soft and still, but live, on a window curtain"). It is also possible to imagine many of the scenes on stage, given how much dialogue there is. But only in fiction could Walker have given us the nuances of thought and especially feeling that are central here. By keeping what dramatic events do occur mostly offstage (the boy's suicide has already taken place when the novel opens, the mountain hike is reported afterward), the author keeps our attention where she wants it: not on the events themselves, but on her characters' responses to those events.

I'm tempted to say that in this way *The Body of a Young Man* seems very much a novel written by a woman—not because I can't think of male writers who are as much interested in interiors, but because I think most of them—except, perhaps, Henry James—would have included more of the external action Walker resolutely resists. This is a novel so beautifully quiet we can hear tiny shifts in the relationship of the characters to themselves, each other, and the world. Reading it is like looking into a clear mountain stream and seeing not only the rocks and leaves, but the shadow of the water itself, as the wind ripples it.

". . . his affection . . . had in no way diminished but there, like the body of a young man laid up in peat for a century, with the red fresh on his lips, was his friendship, in its acuteness and its reality laid up across the bay among the sandhills."

—VIRGINIA WOOLF

One

THE ROAD curved so often there was no clear view ahead. It twisted on itself in wide loops or dropped abruptly into a sunless green hollow between close-growing trees and coarse brakes. From the mulch of fern rot and leaf mold under the trees sprang sturdy ground pine and fleshy toadstools. In one hidden place maidenhair ferns, delicate and easily broken, stirred on their black-lacquered stems. Beyond the hollow the road climbed again into the pale sunshine that washed across green meadows, weather-bleached barns, and white houses, but it was still so narrow that ferns and witch grass brushed against the side of the car, and there was no place to turn around and go back.

Quiet had fallen on the occupants of the car. Even the whirring of the plastic windmill Harp had been holding out the car window was still. They were almost there. Phyllis glanced quickly at James. His eyes were on the road ahead, his lips tight on an unlighted cigarette. He looked tired, she thought.

"What?" he asked.

It was hard to look at anyone beside you in the car without his being aware of it. She reached outside her thoughts to say, "You're getting excited about seeing them, aren't you?"

James's face lighted. "Yes, I really am. Well, you know how I feel about them."

"I know." He had told her about Josh and Lucy Blair the second time she had seen him.

James pushed the lighter back in the dashboard. "There's something psychic about his calling up just when I . . . just then."

3

She wondered what James had started to say and then had stopped, perhaps because of Harp in the back seat. They were careful how much Harp heard them talk about that boy. But then, they did not talk about the boy any more themselves, although she could often feel James thinking about him. She was thankful that she had phoned Josh even though it had seemed like an act of treachery to call him without James knowing it. It had been easy to talk to Josh. He seemed to understand so quickly.

"I know Jim," Josh had said. "He'd feel he was to blame even though he wasn't in the least. That's the way he is." The very timbre of his voice had made her feel better. And Josh had known what to do. "I'll make an excuse for calling him later tonight; I'll tell him I just wanted to hear him, which I do." She had had no thought that the talk would end in their coming here.

"Come and spend the summer with us," Lucy had written in her firm round handwriting. "We're practically isolated up here on our hilltop and your coming will be the salvation of our summer. You know how long we've been trying to get you here! You can have the funny little guesthouse that was once an extra barn and be as independent as calves in clover just across the orchard from us." Laughter seemed to come through the letter.

"There's no one like them," James said now.

"What's the big boy's name?" Harp swooped forward, putting his head between his father and mother and bringing with him a sharp fragrance of spearmint gum.

"Richard," James told him. "They call him Rich. He's sixteen and he probably won't have too much time for small fry like you, Harp, so take it easy at first, but the girl is four years younger, just about your age, in fact. Her name's Ellie." They had told Harp all this before, but re-telling was a way of getting them used to being here. Phyllis said again, "Won't it be splendid, Harp, to have someone your own age to do things with."

"Don't worry, old sobersides," James said, grinning at him in the mirror. At the epithet, Harp grabbed James around the neck so she had to remonstrate. James pretended

4

to be choking and made a realistic gasp that sent Harp into shrieks of laughter. Phyllis glanced at each familiar dial on the dashboard of the car with sudden affection. Simply the coming here to see Josh and Lucy had lifted James's spirits.

"Cut it out now, Harp, we're almost to the village. You have to be dignified in a New England town. I'll stop here and phone 'em, Phyl, and see if we can take the mail out or anything. That's the way we always used to do."

Harp went with James into the general store while Phyllis waited in the car. She could see Harp asking questions as he tagged along. James nodded to the old man on the store steps as though he knew him. She was glad to have this delay before they got there. Now that they were so close, she wondered how it would be to visit someone for the summer. Not visit, exactly, but still . . . not be quite living their own life. James had said that Josh and Lucy were different from anyone else, and they were; different from anyone she had ever known. That time she met them they had been so casual and yet excited about seeing James again, and their excitement had taken her in, too. There was a kind of sparkle about them that removed them from all dull or tired or commonplace people. Lucy was handsome, with her deep blue eyes and her black hair worn severely back from a serene face. And Josh was so . . . exuberant and warm and sure. It was remembering the way he had put his arm around James, as she had seldom seen a man do, that made her call him.

James must be having trouble reaching them, he was so long. It was odd to be here in this village James had told her about so many times; odd to lay the present picture over the one already in her mind. White house for white house, then a brick one; a fan window over a chaste white door, small-paned windows, doorsteps, and elm trees arching over the street. A real New England village, James had said. The white splinter of a steeple pierced the green trees above the houses, but you couldn't see the top from down here in the street because of the heavy leaves.

These houses had come before the jig-saw, cupola, and

porch style she had known in Illinois. Yet how would you play dolls on a hot summer afternoon without a porch? or sit on the swing and talk? The white doors were all closed here. Inside, the parlors must be cool, small but cool. This was the way she had imagined the village as a background for James and Lucy and Josh. They used to come up from college to ski, and stopped here at this very store to get supplies. Or they came in summer. She always saw them laughing, except the time James had told her about when Lucy's father had died, and James had come because he was like one of Lucy's family. "You know," James had told her, "I believe it was hardest on Josh. He just couldn't take it." She remembered that because her mother had died the year before. She had said stupidly, "What else could he do?" "Oh, he did in time, of course; I mean at first," James had explained a little impatiently.

James came out with a bag of peanuts. "I couldn't get them. They're probably off outdoors some place and couldn't hear the phone." He glanced down the street as though he were greeting every single house and granite hitching post. "Isn't it great, Phyl? You'll know this village before the summer's out. Wait'll you see the haircut Harp and I'll get in that barbershop. I wonder if old Hank Foster's still the barber. I didn't think it would ever take me fifteen years to get back here."

Did he mind that it had taken so long? As they drove out of the village, Phyllis studied the houses.

When they passed an old brick house, James said, "That's just a mile from Josh's. I used to think I'd like to own it some day."

"Let's," she said, as though they could go ahead and buy any house they wanted.

"All right," James agreed. "We'll take down that shed, though."

"There's a good barn. We won't need the shed."

"Have to get at that orchard. Look at the dead trees in there."

"Are you going to buy it, Dad? Are you?" Harp demanded.

6

"Well, not right away, but we might," James said.

"He's fooling, isn't he, Mom?" Harp asked.

"Why, we're buying it right now with our eyes," she told him. "Pretend you've moved in and are looking out from the window of your room at this car going by."

Harp stared dubiously at the house, then he said, "The car has three people in it, and it's got a Illinois license on it."

There was another green curve before James said, "That's their mailbox," and turned the car up the steep hill to the house. It was just as she had seen it in James's snapshots: a big old yellow house with a porch around two sides, standing high on a hill.

James touched the horn, and the sound brayed against the quiet summer afternoon. Then he let out a great roar: "We made it!" But no sound came from the house, and the screen door did not move.

"That's funny," James said. "Let's get out."

"We'll be waiting for you. Hurry along," they had said last night when James phoned.

"Let's go in." James held the screen door open.

"Oh, I don't like to do that," Phyllis said and hung back, yet was drawn by the cool hall that led out again at the other end, and the glimpse of the room on the right. A book lay open on the arm of a chair, and one yellow curtain was caught back by an old copper pitcher to let in more air. But she hardly let her eyes rest on these things.

"Maybe they're down getting the guesthouse fixed up," James said as they stepped out on the flagstones at the back of the house. "Let me show you where you get the best view on the place. There! Look across the meadow at the mountain. That's the densest timber! A man got lost up there one summer. Josh and I went with a bunch to find him. Crazy tenderfoot!" He sounded like Harp, she thought.

They walked out a little way from the house. James broke a spray from a bush that grew against the wall. "Smell." The fragrance was new to her, almost too pungent.

"What is it?"

"Lemon verbena."

"I thought that was Southern, along with wistaria and crepe myrtle."

"Nope. New England as lilacs."

"Of course lilacs aren't just New England; they're just as much Middle Western," she reminded him, but James said, "Look where Harp is. He's way down there exploring. Why don't you sit here, Phyl, and I'll go down and look around with Harp."

She couldn't sit still, so she walked around the house. That was when she saw the tall lanky boy coming up the hill. She could not see his face clearly from where she stood, only his head and thin neck and T-shirt-covered shoulders. She swallowed nervously, and one hand closed tight on the spray of verbena so that its spicy odor sharpened the air. For a moment he had seemed like the boy . . .

"Hello!" he shouted, and came running. "We didn't expect you before five. Mother and Dad went to town; they'll be sunk to think they missed you." His smile reminded her of Josh's. "I was just down opening a beaver dam for the sixteenth time. And I almost caught a muskrat."

"You must be Rich," she said, angry with herself for having thought he was like that boy. He spoke the particular language of an Eastern school that had sounded on her ear with such charm the first time she met James. The boy's voice had been flat and slurred. "That's for de chief to decide," he had said. She winced now remembering how he had called James the chief. "James will be so glad to see you," she said. "He and Harpswell went exploring."

"Mother and Dad were sure that if you did come early they'd see you on the road," Rich explained.

"Well, this way we had a chance to look at the view; it's beautiful. You're up so high here." She walked over toward the stone wall so she could look down across the meadow. James and Harp were on their way back. "There's James, and that's Harp," she said to Rich. "James!" she called out, waving to him so he wouldn't see this boy too suddenly, but her voice was lost in the sound of the gravel as Josh and Lucy drove into the yard.

8

Two

IT WAS STRANGE to wake in this guesthouse; almost
a relief, as if she were separated from her own living for a
while. She lay still and watched the light of a summer morning poke at the shadows of the room and find the washstand
and the wooden side of the old blanket chest. The bareness
of the room pleased her. There were no photographs on the
wall. No picture of her mother, for whom life had been brief
and not too happy and who used to say, "You want to be
awfully sure whom you give your heart to, Phyllis!" No
picture of her father, whom she knew better by his handwriting than by his voice. He had made her cautious about
believing in someone, until she met James. At home, the baby
picture of Harp on the wall had come to bother her. She
wanted to keep him smiling just as he was there, right up
through adolescence into maturity. But no one could do
that for anyone. It was almost a relief not to have the picture of James that she had always loved. When she looked at
it, she kept seeing that it didn't have the lines of strain and
sadness she now saw sometimes on his face. Terrible to look
at early pictures and know what was ahead of each of those
vulnerable faces. But as though those familiar pictures all
hung on these thin plasterboard walls, she saw each one.
She looked away from them to James on the cot by the wall.

"You'll probably hate having separate beds; we do,"
Lucy had said. "But these are all we had. Maybe you can
manage." Her smile was humorous and gentle and encom-
passed both their lives. "Besides, I know you would never
forgive me if I didn't let you take things just as they are,
so I haven't done an extra thing."

That was the condition that had made it possible to come.

9

They could be here a while and really not feel that they were upsetting Lucy's and Josh's lives, not putting them out. Jámes had said last night, "Thank goodness for people who are relaxed. There aren't many in the world, I'm beginning to think. Not like Lucy and Josh."

She thought again of the way Lucy had put her arms around her and said, "Oh, Phyllis, I'm glad you've come." And Josh had kissed her and said, "We've waited too long for this visit." What good friends they were. She had never known friends like these. When James used to talk about Josh, she always felt he exaggerated. "I don't suppose there was anything I thought about that Josh didn't know, and I knew pretty much how Josh felt about things. You know?" She didn't.

Instead of getting up as she had meant to and walking across the meadow toward the mountain, she stretched her arms up above her head. How did you really relax? Like a cat, someone had said. She tried it, tried feeling her limbs heavy against the sheet, moving her mind out away from her body, out beyond the window so it was an emptiness of green leaves and light early-morning sky, without even a green thought. Nothing was wrong. James had been depressed, naturally, because he cared so much about the boy, but Josh would make him see that the boy's death wasn't his fault. She could leave him to Josh. She turned her head so she could see into the trees that grew close to the house.

There was a sound in the next small room, where Harp slept. She heard him open the front door. Then she saw him walking past the window, not looking in for fear he would be seen. She could remember that feeling. He must be going across the orchard to find Rich and go for the milk in the jeep. How thoughtful of Lucy to ask him for breakfast so she and James could be lazy this first morning. As long as James slept, she would lie still. But she kept listening for the sound of the big buses stopping at the corner at home, and the squeal of tires on the boulevard one block over. It took time to get used to country stillness. This was different from being at a cottage at the lake. And it was greener than any place she had ever been; all she could see from the window were layers on layers of green leaves.

The jeep made enough noise to wake anyone.

Something moved on the opposite wall where the sun threw a bright rectangle of light. Then she saw it was the shadow of James's head. He was lying on his back staring straight ahead of him. Maybe he wasn't worrying, though. Maybe he was listening to that bird out there in the green leaves, or had just waked when he heard the jeep.

"Good morning." She went across to James's bed and sat down on the edge. His quick smile covered over the sober expression of his face.

"Morning, dear," he said. "Welcome to my bed."

James hadn't had this light tone in . . . weeks, but she only said, "Move your head; I need more pillow."

"You don't need a pillow at all; try that." He pulled her head down against his bare shoulder. "Think you'll like it here?"

"I like it already. How many summers were you here, James?"

"Five or six . . . six, I guess, but we always came up in the winter when we were in college, you know; Josh and I. When Lucy was in Europe, her mother invited us up. It's like home to me."

"I feel as though I'd known them a long time, too," she said. "They're wonderful." She felt so good to lie this minute in James's arm and hear the lift in his voice.

"I saw Harp creep past the window a little while ago. He'll have a great time," James said. He had been awake then. After a moment, Phyllis slid out of bed.

"You stay here and I'll bring you a cup of coffee. Unless you want to go out in the sun. We can walk right into an orchard."

When the coffee was ready, she went out of the house through the grass in her gown. The trees were so old and angular they seemed to have broken out of their regular rows to stand in groups; and she could see tiny green knobs of apples.

11

"It's heavenly out here, James," she called. "Come and see." She was bothered that he didn't call back. "If you want any coffee, you'll have to come out and get it." She poured her own and set the pot on a flat stone on top of the wall.

James appeared in the doorway. He still wore no top, and his skin looked too pale, as though it had taken on the unhealthy sallowness of his thoughts, but when he came across the grass, the sun touched it with warm color. He gave a long, low whistle. "Nice, pretty nice," he said. "I'm glad you got me out."

Then they heard Josh calling to them. "If ever I saw Adam and Eve in the garden!" When he stepped up on the stone wall, he looked bigger than any mere man.

"Oh, Josh, I'm not very well clad. I just couldn't resist walking right outside in the sun," Phyllis said.

"Don't move! You look to me like a demure young girl in a dimity gown; no, a shepherdess under a tree. How's that, Jim?"

"Smooth, boy. You haven't lost your touch," James told him.

"Who said anything about touch? Eyes are all I'm using." In the burst of laughter under the trees, Phyllis escaped to the house.

"Look, you've frightened her away, you serpent!" Josh complained. "Phyllis, come back. Remember all that trouble in the garden started over clothes."

"I won't put on too many and I'll be back in a minute and bring you a cup of hot coffee," Phyllis called back. She had never known such gay fooling with anyone but James.

"I couldn't wait any longer to see how you slept your first night in the old barn," Josh said when she came back. "Lucy gave me strict orders to get to work and write at least half a chapter before I came over here, but I sneaked off."

"Josh, are you writing a book?" Phyllis asked.

Josh shrugged and made a wry face. "Sometimes I think I am, sometimes not. As a matter of fact, Jim, I've had an ulterior motive in getting you up here. I'm going to get you to read it and see what you think of it."

"Well, you really got at it!" James said. "That one on Lucretius you were muttering about?"

"No, I'm still going to do that one; I've got four or five chapters of it that I've used for lectures, but this is something the dean and a couple of alumni seem to think I ought to write." He reached over and pulled a long stalk of timothy to chew before he went on. "Sort of a collection of the things I've been saying . . . you know, talks, advice I've been doling out over the years." Josh threw away the stalk of grass and took up his coffee cup. "They seem to think some of the stuff has been useful . . ." he mumbled.

"What you have to say about Lucretius would be, too, I imagine," James said. "Wait'll I get some cigarettes."

"I'll get them for you," Phyllis said. "I'm going in to get some breakfast and then you can both come." As she went toward the house, she heard Josh saying, "Why don't you give up smoking, Jim? You've got a regular thing about it. I haven't smoked since a year ago last summer."

"Still the old reformer!" James jibed. "Didn't you learn years ago that I don't reform easily?"

They were like two boys together, she thought. She moved out of the green shadow of the orchard into the bright sun, and went on into the house.

"Hey, where are those cigarettes, Phyl?" James called. "You two must be in a conspiracy."

Three

"JOSHUA BLAIR, you went over and woke them the very first morning!" Lucy said with mock severity. "I saw you going through the orchard and I knew very well." She piled the wet lettuce in a wire basket and swung it like an incense burner over the altar of the soapstone sink. The morning sun caught the drops of water that flew off the scalloped leaves.

"They were already up; they were having coffee out in the orchard." Josh looked too big for the small kitchen chair as he sat astride it, his arms on the top of the spindled back. "He's different from last night," Josh said.

"That's not surprising. Last night Jim was excited at seeing us after such a long time. He's been under a strain. Give him time to get rested and let down." Josh was like this when the children were sick or cross, always impatient to have them back to normal. It was a lucky thing she was healthy; he would have suffered too much over an invalid wife.

"Any more coffee?" Josh asked.

She filled the big pottery cup without answering. In this house there was always more coffee, more bread, more room, more children or friends. Josh liked abundance. He liked giving. Now he wanted to help Jim, of course. How good he was!

But he hardly tasted his coffee before he set down the cup. "Jim isn't himself. He has flashes . . . you know? And sparks over something, and then, the next minute, he seems to be preoccupied with his own thoughts. He's really taken this boy's death to heart."

14

"I don't think that's strange," Lucy said slowly. "You know how sensitive Jim is. Did he say anything about it?"

"Not in so many words, but I could see that it was in his mind. And . . ."

She waited, looking out the window at the gentle line of mountain beyond the meadow.

". . . I told him about the book, you know." Her eyes came back to him. His hand moved over the top of the chair back as though testing its smoothness. "I was telling him the kind of thing I was doing, and he said, 'How can you be sure of the advice you give? Maybe it's the worst thing you could tell them.'"

"What did you say?"

Josh shrugged his shoulders. "I said you could only give the advice that seemed best to you. It must be pretty fair or they wouldn't keep coming back to talk with me. . . ."

"But, Josh, don't you see that he feels he gave the wrong advice. Isn't that what Phyllis said? The boy . . ."

"Jim was probably so interested in seeing that boy get ahead he didn't really analyze him closely enough to understand what he was like."

"Yet I can't imagine Jim not understanding." She thought of the time her father died. Jim had known so exactly how she felt. "Don't say that to him, Josh," she said quickly.

"I'm not going to say anything to him till I've had a chance to talk to Phyl. I like her, don't you? I remembered her as being rather quiet, but this morning she was out in the orchard in her gown, and gay as a sprite."

"So you approve of her now!" She smiled at him, thinking how he had stormed over Jim's marrying her. "You didn't think anybody was good enough for Jim," she teased. "And, of course, he felt the same way about your marrying me."

"Lucy, that isn't true and you know it. Jim would have married you himself if I hadn't made you promise to marry me first." Josh was serious sometimes when she expected him to joke about something.

15

"Silly!" she said quickly but wondering about it. Then she went back to Jim and Phyllis. "They're very close to each other, Josh, I can see that."

The jeep came grinding up the driveway and Josh went out to the porch to meet it. Ellie jumped down, but Harp sat beside Rich.

She heard Harp ask, "Can I ride over to the barn, Rich, can I?" and heard Rich say, "Sure, if you want to. You want to carry the cans over to the porch first?" Rich was good at organizing people to help him. Already he had Harp lined up.

"I'll ride down with you." Josh climbed into the jeep and they drove off to the barn.

"Nice to have another boy here, isn't it, Ellie?"

"Mmm." Ellie sucked the end of one of her braids. "He's younger than me."

"*I*, Ellie, not *me*. He seems old for his age to me." She took care to drop the thought into Ellie's mind.

"He reads a lot," Ellie offered. "When I told him the cat was named Magwitch, he knew right away that his name came out of *Great Expectations*. And he got into an awful argument with Rich, Mother, 'cause he said he guessed he'd read at least a hundred books, all grown-up ones. Rich said he didn't believe it. He could have, couldn't he?"

"Perhaps."

"Mother?"

"Yes."

"I don't know whether he really tells the truth, though."

"Why, Ellie?" There was no use trying to stop Ellie once she was started on some thought, but she began picking up the breakfast dishes.

"Because when we came over the bridge, down by the mill, you know, Rich told him about how the bridge is haunted because of that crazy man that jumped off, way, way back, and was drowned."

Why would Rich tell such a thing? She would talk to Rich.

"Well, Harp said he knew a boy that jumped off a bridge and drowned himself. He said that Uncle Jim taught him

16

in school and he'd even been at their house for dinner lots of times. He was making it up, wasn't he? He couldn't have really known anybody like that, could he?"

"I suppose he could have, Ellie." If she kept her voice calm and disinterested, maybe Ellie would forget all this more quickly. "But I wouldn't ever ask him about it."

Ellie's eyes were dark with thinking. Her mouth pursed.

"Do you hear, Ellie?" Her voice sounded stern in spite of her.

Ellie nodded. Without being told, she picked up the towel and started to wipe the dishes. "Can I ask you one thing?"

"Of course."

"Do you think the boy wanted to drown?"

"Ellie, I don't know, and we haven't any right to try to guess."

"But Mother, it makes it worse if he really did mean to drown."

Lucy let the water run noisily into the dishpan for a minute. Better not to say anything more. Ellie wiped silently at the white syrup pitcher with the little green leaves on it. She couldn't tell what the child was thinking. She heard her catch her breath and the crash of the pitcher on the floor. Ellie's eyes filled with tears.

"Never mind. Pick up the pieces," she said briskly. Now Ellie would *never* forget the boy who drowned. His death would always be mixed with the broken pitcher. There was a diabolical will in things. She had always felt that was true.

From the big window over the sink, she could see Harp and Rich coming up from the barn with Josh. Josh was explaining something to Harp, who was smiling. How fine for the boy to be here with Josh this summer; good for Phyllis and Jim, too.

Josh came to the screen door. "What's the matter with Ellie?"

Lucy answered, "Oh, nothing. She just dropped the syrup pitcher."

"That's not too bad, Ellie. Put it in my study and I'll see if I can't mend it," Josh said.

17

She was relieved to see Ellie smile. "You can run along, dear, I'm going to drain the rest," she told her.

"Lu, let's ask Jim and Phyl for dinner tonight, and cook outside," Josh suggested.

"Fine," Lucy agreed, as she usually did to Josh's ideas. Then she said, "Maybe we should let them feel they are independent first. I thought I'd take Phyl to the village with me for groceries and let her get set up."

"I thought you stocked the place before they came? And they can have all the fresh vegetables they want. They won't need . . ."

"I know, Josh, but they'll feel we're doing too much if you're not careful."

Josh exploded. "Jim and Phyl aren't like that. They ought to know they're as welcome as . . ." She looked at him warningly as Harp came into the kitchen.

Four

THE FIRST SUNDAY they were there was Ellie's twelfth birthday. That morning, Harp had brought down Lucy's invitation to supper. "And we're going to eat outdoors and have fireworks afterward even if it *is* only the first of July. Uncle Josh says so," he announced. Phyllis sent him back to ask Lucy if she could make a cake with strawberry icing for the occasion. She and Lucy might have been neighbors living in a village . . . no, two children playing house across the orchard from each other.

And in the evening the two families sat around the table, out on the flagstones. ("*Don't* call it a terrace, for Heaven's sake!" Josh had warned.) Red, white, and blue streamers ran the length of the white cloth, and from the lowest branch of the maple trees in front of the house hung balloons, losing their color now in the slow-coming dusk.

"What a gay idea that is," Phyllis had said when she saw the balloons.

"We always do that for birthdays," Lucy told her. "Remember, Jim, we hung them for you one time in February."

"Indeed I do. I looked out of the window in the morning and couldn't believe my eyes."

What fun they must have had. Phyllis looked at the dark trees and could almost see them bare with the balloons hanging above the snow.

"Happy birthday to you . . ." Lucy began as she set the cake down in front of Ellie. Josh boomed the words way out across the meadow. Rich's voice cracked on the high note, but they all finished together—"Happy birthday to you!"

Ellie bit her lip and stared at the candles. She was like

Lucy, Phyllis thought, looking at her dark hair and her blue eyes, lit now by the twelve little candle flames on the strawberry cake.

"Blow, Ellie, quick, or the frosting'll melt!" Harp said.

"I have to decide on my wish," she told him, flashing her eyes at him. In the waiting it was so silent they could hear the brook running.

"Oh come on!" Rich said, his voice deep against Ellie's and Harp's.

"I can't be sure what to wish," Ellie wailed.

"It's not so tragic as all that, Puss," Josh said. Phyllis caught Lucy's glance of mock hopelessness. After you were older, you knew so well what to wish for, she thought. She wished now for just one thing, to have James free from the horrible shadow of that boy's death. She felt guilty to be hanging a desperate grown-up wish on a child's birthday candle.

"Well, blow!" Harp stormed in disgust. "You prob'ly won't get it anyway."

Ellie's eyes moved around the table, imploring.

"You don't have to tell your wish," Lucy reminded her.

"To myself I do," Ellie insisted. Her eyes fell suddenly on James. "I wish," she said slowly, "that Uncle Jim will stay here all summer." Then she blew, holding her breath till the candles were out and the burned smell floated on the air.

"Why, Ellie!" Quick tears stung Phyllis's eyes. She glanced over at James.

"Thank you, Ellie," he said. "I've got to stay anyway till you show me where that circle of Indian pipes is." He smiled at her as though they had a secret together.

"You're going to help me take the transmission apart, Jim," Rich reminded him. "Dad says I'll never get it together again."

"I didn't promise we would get it together, Rich. I promised to help you take it apart."

There was always something between James and children, Phyllis thought. At high school . . . then she remembered how that boy had almost worshiped James.

"Come on, Uncle Jim, let's set off my fireworks!" Ellie urged.

"Dad, you said I could do some of them," Harp begged.

"Rich is going to be master of ceremonies, Harp. We'll have to wait and see what he'll let us do," James said, getting up to go. Phyllis watched him. Ellie and Harp ran ahead and Rich walked with James, and again Rich reminded her too strongly of that boy. She had watched the boy and James go off like this from the house so often.

"You see how we all feel about your being here," Josh said.

"I'm so glad we came," Phyllis answered. "You don't know how I hesitated to call you; it seemed a terrible thing to do without James's knowing, but there wasn't anyone else I could go to. . . ." She was ashamed that she was so close to tears.

"You shouldn't have hesitated a minute," Lucy murmured.

Josh went over and raised the awning. "Let's have the whole night sky to see the fireworks in," he said. Phyllis leaned her head against the back of the chair and looked far up into the gentle darkness. There was so much room here, room to breathe, and none of that loneliness she remembered as a girl, sitting on the porch in Chicago on a summer evening.

Josh came back and sat down beside her. "While we have a chance, Phyl, tell me a little more about Jim. I can see he's still brooding about that boy's death, but you've been here more than a week and he still doesn't seem to want to talk about it with me. Over the phone, you know, he said, 'I've been through a hell of a thing here. One of the boys I taught committed suicide.' That's all he said. Shall I ask him about it, or shall I wait till he says something himself?"

"I don't really know, Josh. He doesn't talk about it to me any more, yet I can feel him worrying about it all the time." She didn't want to say that sometimes he walked for hours . . . just walked and came home tired out and then didn't sleep, or that some nights he didn't come to bed until it was light enough to see the clock on his dresser. And when she had said the boy's death wasn't his fault, he had turned on her almost angrily . . . James, who was never angry with her, and said, "Don't say that, Phyllis. He'd be living today if I hadn't put him up against more than he could take." Now she said, "Sometimes I can't seem to reach him."

The first skyrocket shot up into the sky with a soft pfht sound and burst into unreal shapes of light, though no more unreal than her sitting here saying such things about James.

Josh's chair scraped harshly against the flagstones. The light from the kitchen window shone on his face. He looked older than he had that first morning. With his glasses off, the fine lines about his eyes showed. It was a strong face and one she could trust.

"As I said to you that night over the phone, Phyl, Jim's the kind who'd go on bedeviling himself. Was there much publicity about the thing?"

"Oh yes, for a couple of days. The papers came out with headlines. . . ." She couldn't speak for an instant, seeing them again, screaming from the paper, BODY OF A YOUNG MAN FOUND DROWNED. . . . She had hidden the clipping in the bottom drawer of the desk. "The whole school was shocked, of course. James came home looking terrible. Harp said they were talking about it at his school. James went right down to see the boy's family. They blamed him. They said the boy never really wanted to go on to college, that it was all because of James. I . . . I went to see them, too." She saw again the front door with the card above the bell that said "bell out of order go to shop." She had gone and found the boy's father working the big pressing iron in his shop.

"I know your husband feel terrible, Missus Cutler, but that don't bring back our son. He thought everything your husband said he had to do. It was too much for him." Phyllis closed her eyes now to try to get the picture of the old man out of her mind.

"Of course, this sort of thing could happen to me," Josh was saying. "I've advised boys to try for scholarships; it just happened that they had the stuff."

The next rocket shot like a green-and-yellow bird into the warm night sky, finding its way between two stars. They could hear the children shouting. Then James's voice came back to them: "Wasn't that a beauty, Ellie? Must have carried your wish right to the moon." His voice lifted Phyllis's spirits.

"Hear him, Phyl?" Lucy said as though she were talking to Ellie. "He'll be all right again. Now that he's here, he'll forget all about it. I'm going to get out the ice cream. You stay here and talk with Josh."

Phyllis was glad that Lucy had gone; it was easier to talk with Josh alone.

"Of course, he'll get over this," Josh said. "He's too strong, he has too much sense, to go to pieces over a thing like that." He laid his hand over hers on the chair arm. The tenderness was too much for her.

"Oh, Josh, I've been so worried about him." In spite of herself, she was crying. "I'm sorry," she said, trying to stop.

"Nothing to be sorry about. I can understand just how you feel. I'm going to get Jim to work helping me build that wall out there and reading my manuscript. . . . I'm glad he's away from that place where everything reminds him of the thing. I never thought he should spend his life teaching there, anyway."

"You don't know how grateful I am, Josh," she said in a low voice. She watched a fountain of color shoot into the soft darkness and then cascade in wide spirals and fall somewhere in the meadow. "I couldn't talk about James to anybody else . . . to anybody who didn't love him," she finished, her voice faltering on the word "love."

"I understand that," Josh said. And then he added, "If Lucy were worried about me, I'd expect her to go to Jim. You know how Jim and I feel about each other. It's the kind of rare understanding you don't often find, I guess."

23

This was another world, she thought. A better world than she had known in her childhood. James was part of it, and Josh, and Lucy, and now she belonged to it.

"That's all! That was the last of 'em," Josh said.

James and the children began to sing as they came back up the hill. "Jimmy crack corn and I don't care. . . ." Josh went down to meet them. The night was gentle and safe. Fireflies flashed above the darkness of the tiger lilies and then were lost behind the lilac bush. From the pond below the house, the rasp of the frogs rose comically under the long-drawn and melancholy notes "My Master's gone away. . . ."

Phyllis leaned back in her chair. What if she hadn't called Josh!

"You put on a real exhibition!" Josh said as James and the children came back to the porch.

"Did you see the fountain, Mom, did you see it?" Harp asked. "I set that off."

"No, sir, Harp, not alone. I did it, too!" Ellie insisted.

Above the clamor, Lucy asked, "Who'll have some ice cream?" And then she said to Josh, "The pump's off again, Josh. You'll have to go to Staples the first thing in the morning and see if you can get it fixed again."

"The pump!" James exclaimed. "If that doesn't sound like old times. Phyl, as long as I can remember the pump was breaking down and we were always dashing to Staples to get it fixed. I'd be sunk if you ever got a new one."

Five

"THE PLEASANT PART about having a guesthouse is that your friends are there but you have your meals by yourselves when you want them," Lucy said the next morning, smiling across the table at Josh. He and Rich had been up at five and gone to the Quarry hole for a dip before breakfast. "Finish the pancakes, Rich, I've got a whole plate coming up."

"You sit down, I'll get these," Josh said. He flipped them in the air with a practiced hand and brought them steaming hot to the table. Lucy had to cover her plate with both hands to keep him from filling it. She sat drinking her coffee and watching them eat. Jim's paleness, his quietness had made her more aware of Josh's healthy tan and his high spirits. She had never appreciated them so much.

"You eat another, yourself, Josh," she said, and was pleased when he took two.

Harp appeared in the doorway.

"Come in, young man," Josh said. "Have a chair and some of the best pancakes you ever ate." Harp grinned and slid into one of the armchairs that looked too big for his slight body. "Are your mother and father up or are you the only early bird?"

"They're still asleep," Harp said.

"Well, that's good for these old folks, but we young things don't need much sleep, do we?" Josh liked to emphasize his youth, Lucy thought with amusement, but then, he *was* young.

"Who's coming with me to Staples to get the pump fixed? I have an idea we just may break down and buy a new one. You're coming with us, aren't you, Lucy?" Josh asked.

"Oh, I can't this morning, Josh. I think I'll weave. You know I want to get so much done this summer."

He looked at her in mock reproach. "Penelope, you're sure you don't unravel every night what you've done in the day time?"

She knew he was disappointed as he went down the hill toward the barn, but it was good for him to have the children and Rich to himself. Besides, she meant to keep a piece of each day for her own this summer.

Inside the old woodshed, the small checks of sun fell across the warped plank floor like an unrolled bolt of gingham, but when she let the upper half of the lattice swing back, the full sun erased the checks, picking out the green and yellow and lavender threads on the big loom that had been her grandmother's. Lucy slid on the bench and studied the pattern of color in front of her.

As she threw the shuttle, she felt her mind settle. To make something whole out of the separate threads always smoothed and ordered her thoughts, and she could think freely when she wove. Afterward, looking at the pattern, she could remember some of the things she had thought, or how Josh had come in to talk, or the time she had been sick, or the day the shed had been too damp to sit in but she had stayed there anyway. Even knowing that Jim and Phyllis Cutler were coming, and that there wouldn't be much time this month, she had started a new piece. Josh teased her about her weaving, but he knew the way she felt about it—the way he did about building up all the fallen-down stone walls on the place. And he was always proud of what she had made. Her mouth curved thinking of the way he said to people, "My wife made these mats on the same loom her grandmother used, a handmade loom, out of solid cherry."

She had been pleased with the pattern in the beginning, but in the bright light this morning, it looked too . . . delicate and pastel. It needed something sharper. Black would be too much of a contrast. Across, on the wall, on the shallow shelves, stood the spools of thread, making a Roman-striped band against the boards. The spools always

26

smelled of the wood that had been piled there in other years, and she sometimes caught the old wood scent as the thread followed the shuttle. Why not blue? That dark, almost garish blue that she had bought but never used.

She let her hand slip back and forth four times, watching to see the new color strike against the green. It altered the green, made it grayer, but brought out the yellow. She sat still a long moment, holding the shuttle motionless in her hand.

What was it about Jim? It wasn't that he moped around. He had gone off to play tennis with Rich yesterday, and the other afternoon he had taken Ellie and Harp berrying, but he seemed removed from them all. Josh wanted so much to help him that it was hard for him to wait until Jim was ready to talk to him. That was the way Josh was; he was sure something could be done. When students got into difficulty, someone always said, "Go see Josh Blair; he'll know what to do." When Josh was closeted in the study with some boy, she knew that when the boy left he would come out either wrapped up in his problem or exhilarated by feeling he had found a way to solve it. But this was different.

Without stopping to look back at the loom, she went out of the shed and down across the orchard to the guest-house.

"Phyl, I thought it would be larky to have some people in for supper tonight. Come go with me to town to invite them. Just come as you are." She had an uncomfortable feeling that Phyllis had been sitting there not doing anything. Oh, maybe she was reading. Phyllis looked younger in her shirt and jeans. Her light hair, cut straight like a child's, and her lashes as pale as the freckles on her white skin showed off better in clothes like these. Her eyes were light brown in her oval face. She could sit for a painting by Modigliani; even her hands and wrists were thin enough. Except that she was fair.

"From your letter, I thought you were completely isolated here," Phyllis said as they walked over to the car.

"Well, we are, more or less, but we see a few people. The

Downeys have a summer place. He's a professional photographer, rather fun because he's been every place and photographed all kinds of people. His wife looks oriental . . . loveliest skin and eyes." She was rattling, but that was all right. "Tom Blake is the doctor in the village. His wife's a real New Englander, and she has a wonderful old house that's been in her family since 1694. Josh thinks the house is what keeps Tom here, but you know Josh. He's so impatient if everyone isn't stretching every nerve and pressing with vigor on." Would that make Phyllis think Josh was impatient with James? What a stupid thing for her to say.

But Phyllis only said, "You have variety, anyway."

"Josh really loves having people around, and James used to enjoy the parties we had up here." The sound of a question got into her voice.

"I'm sure James will like it," Phyllis said, but she didn't sound sure.

"I met Jim the same time I met Josh, you know," Lucy plunged on. "I thought he was the easiest person to talk to I'd ever known." She wasn't quite sure, herself, about where the conversation would lead, but she wanted Phyllis to know how much Jim meant to them.

"I thought that, too," Phyllis said, smiling.

Lucy remembered that weekend she had gone to see Josh at college. She had said to Jim, "Josh is serious about things when I don't expect him to be; he's not exactly . . . gay." And Jim had said, "Oh, he has his light side. They don't come any finer than Joshua Blair, and he needs someone like you." Maybe Jim's saying that, just then, had something to do with her being engaged that spring. Incredible now to remember that she had been so critical. Josh's humor was simply a different kind, which she had come to count on, as she had on his real humanity. He did care more about people than she did, in a way. She couldn't imagine being married to anyone else in the world but Josh.

Phyllis said, "I wish I had known you three then. James has such wonderful stories about you. I used to love to hear them, but I minded, too. I . . ." She laughed in a kind of embarrassment. "I suppose they made me feel left out."

"Good heavens! You certainly don't any more."

"Now that I'm here I don't. I felt rather hesitant about coming, except that I wanted James to be here. It sounds so silly now." She laughed again, a small bodiless laugh.

"You don't know how glad Josh and I are to have a chance to know you at last," Lucy said quickly.

But a thin silence seemed to spread between them. It was unfortunate that Phyllis had said that about being left out; it made them both uncomfortable. Lucy remembered guiltily that Josh had said he wished Jim could come alone for a month, while Phyllis visited her family. And she had reminded him that Phyllis didn't have any family: her mother was dead and her father had been divorced years ago and married again. It would have been better, though, if Jim were here by himself; like old times. Phyllis was an uneasy sort of person. She found herself so aware of her all the time, wondering what she was thinking when she was silent, whether she was having a good time. She wished Phyllis did more, played tennis or painted or something. She just walked or read. That was because she was a librarian, of course.

"Do you still work in the library?" she asked, and then wondered if the question came out abruptly.

"Three days a week, in the children's room," Phyllis said. "The money's useful and I like it."

Now Lucy could see her there, sitting surrounded by small children in a circle listening to her with eager faces.

"Do you tell stories?"

"Yes, one afternoon a week. The rest of the time I'm just at the desk, but I help them find books. Sometimes I can get a child who's only read books about so-and-so's vacation at the seashore . . . you know . . . to read fairy stories."

"Do you think that's better for him?"

Phyllis's eyes seemed to open wider. "Yes, don't you? I couldn't have stood it as a child if I hadn't read fairy stories."

They turned into the main street, and Lucy said with a shade of relief, "Isn't this village street lovely? You know, I've been here every summer of my life."

29

"Lovely," Phyllis echoed. "It makes me think of *Little Women.*"

Lucy tested the remark in her mind, wondering just how Phyllis had meant it.

And that night as they all sat out on the flagstones after supper, Mary Blake asked, "Are you going to be here all summer, Phyllis?"

"Indeed they are. We've made them sign a contract to stay," Lucy answered for her. What abrupt questions people asked, and such awkward ones. "It's the most wonderful break for us. Jim and Josh haven't been together for years, and Phyl and I are just beginning to know each other."

"Your husband must be another of those lucky individuals who teach and have the whole summer to play in," Sam Downey said with a grin at Josh. "Now *I* slave all week and only come up here every other weekend."

"Remarkable the way you get that tan just in weekends, Sam!" Josh said.

"James teaches physics in the high school in Bellevue, Illinois," Phyllis said. "But he usually teaches summer school, too, in a special program they have every summer."

Lucy could see that Sam was taken aback to be answered so flatly.

"Slaves like I do all year, Sam," Josh cut in. "You just can't understand the intensity of the kind of work Jim and I do."

Underneath his fooling, Lucy could see that Josh was making a point of linking Jim's teaching with his own. He had always felt that Jim was wasting himself out there. She glanced over at Jim listening to what Tom Blake was saying and wondered if he felt that way about it.

"You know, Josh, I often wonder how they persuaded you to teach," Lucy said. "Not with any lure of money, that's certain." She picked up Sam's and Phyllis's glasses and followed Josh to the kitchen. Sam had moved his chair over by Phyllis. That was good. But she would be something new for him.

Josh was elated. "Jim and Tom are having a regular old argument, Lu. Jim's forgotten all about his troubles. He's talking physics a mile a minute."

Lucy slid the ice tray back in the refrigerator.

"The thing to do is to get Jim separated from that place out there, particularly after this thing. I'm going to talk to Hopkins about him."

It was like Josh to have a plan, she thought. But he mustn't be in too much of a hurry, before Jim was ready.

The children came back from the movie eight miles away. Lucy heard the parental tone in her own voice as she said, "Hello, dears, was the movie good?" Then the signal to speak politely, "You know these people. . . ." Was it her voice or her mother's, years ago of a summer evening. "I saved some shortcake for you. And there's lots of hot water," she added before she thought, because she caught a faint sweaty smell as Rich went by. She must remember that he was too old for her to suggest such things any longer. "Mary, this is Harpswell Cutler, Phyllis's and Jim's boy." Her hand was on his shoulder as she took him around, and she could feel his slight tensing, the quick little bob of his head, and the reach of his arm to shake hands with the men. When he had finished, he went over to Phyllis for a minute, as though, Lucy felt, he were establishing the fact that Phyllis, not she, could put her hand on his shoulder. That was silly, but she felt he held her off.

"I'm glad you decided not to have Rich go to summer school, Josh." As the children went for their dessert, Tom Blake said, "The worst thing you can do to a boy at this age is to push him, make him feel under pressure," he added, turning to James. "Don't you think so?"

"I quite agree," James said, lighting a fresh cigarette.

"Except that you worry about them idling all summer, too." Lucy put in. "They feel they have to drive all over the country in these crazy old cars, all so souped up. You never know what will happen to them."

"You know," Josh said in his most humorous tone, "I rather think my wife should be called Cassandra."

Somehow the talk went on. Lucy heard Phyllis saying

31

something about Vermont. "James loved it so much when he was in college, I'm glad he can be back here." How could she say that now? Tom couldn't have said anything worse to Jim if he had tried. Without looking at Jim, Lucy was aware that he was sitting silent. She was relieved when the children came back. "The children get along splendidly together," she said in answer to Mary's question. "Practically inseparable." She watched Harp going down toward the guesthouse. He looked lonely and unbearably young. She had said that once to Josh when they were watching Rich, and he had laughed at her. "I never think that. I think of him as Huck Finn when I see him heading off to the woods alone." But Huckleberry Finn was often lonely, she remembered.

Rich added a log to the fire before he sat down on the step by the men to listen to the talk, and her eyes lingered proudly over his grown-up air. Ellie came over to her. "Mother, do I have to go to bed if Rich doesn't?" But there was no conviction behind the question. Lucy leaned close to her ear and whispered about a hot bath and then bed and read a while; it really wasn't very interesting down here, and with a wrinkle of her nose, she sided with Ellie against the adults. Now she could feel Ellie agreeing by the way she moved her body before she said anything.

"I got lots of fresh mosquito bites."

"Well, put some of that lotion on them, dear."

Ellie shook her head. "That's for before it happens. It's no good afterward." And then, as though satisfied with this pronouncement, she went on into the house.

Had Jim heard what Ellie said? "Why don't you and Rich play that new piece you've been practicing on your recorders, Josh?" Lucy asked quickly. Notes were much safer than words.

Everyone fell obediently silent, even though they groaned inwardly as the fluty sounds floated out through the dark to drown in the heavy dew of the lower meadow. Josh played a tenor and Rich a soprano, and it seemed to Lucy that the strains were as separate as their two personalities. Meeting at points and then veering off again.

Rich blew a sour note and recovered, but that, too, was mercifully drowned. She should never have asked them to play.

The minute they were through, Sam Downey said, "Did you see the program the other night on television . . ." She wished they would all go home. Never had she had such a dismal evening. What would Phyl and Jim think?

"You must come down for dinner next week," Mary Blake was saying to Phyllis. "Yes," Tom Blake said. "I want to show you that article, Jim." Lucy was listening for Jim's answer even though she was telling Sam Downey that their tomatoes were going to be larger than his this summer. She missed whatever Jim said.

At last, Hester Downey called out the inevitable, "It's been so much fun. . . ."

Mary said, "A lovely time, Lucy!"

"Come on in and have a nightcap," Josh urged.

"No," James said, "I'm just right," but he lingered to light his cigarette.

"I've got to get down to work tomorrow," Josh said. "You haven't told me what you thought of the first chapter, Jim."

Lucy sighed. Why did Josh ask that now? Unless he wanted to get Jim's mind off the evening. Phyllis was already carrying glasses into the kitchen, but Lucy waited before following her to hear what Jim said. He was so slow in answering he couldn't have liked it, or was he still brooding over what Tom Blake had said?

"I think it must be a difficult kind of book to write, Josh," Jim said finally. "These are sort of philosophical essays intended for undergraduates, I gather?"

"Well, yes, in a way," Josh said. "Not just for undergraduates, either. So many old students have spoken to me about wishing I would put some of the things I've said down. A kind of way of life I suppose they represent, or an attitude toward life would be better." He reached over and picked up Jim's lighter from the table, and tossed it in his hand. "This is the centennial year, you know, and they wanted something of this kind. . . ."

"They're written in your inimitable style, all right." Jim was smiling.

"Well, the style . . . of course, they'll need a lot of polishing." She could see how embarrassed Josh was. He rubbed his finger over the wheel of the lighter.

"No, that's the best thing about them. They have warmth and sincerity. . . ."

Lucy could feel Jim choosing his words carefully.

"You mean you don't care for what they say," Josh cut in.

"Let's say that I'm just a little allergic to the idea of advising young men. I don't believe I'm the one to read them, Josh." Jim lit his cigarette with a match and walked over to the edge of the flagstones to throw it into the shrubbery. When he came back, he said, "I told you over the phone that night you called what had happened to the boy I advised."

Lucy went out then to the kitchen. "Jim's telling Josh about it, Phyl."

"Ah," Phyllis said. "Let me wash because I don't know where the dishes go. It's foolish to leave them till tomorrow."

And although they had had no thought of doing the dishes before, they went to work. Phyllis praised the old milk glass, and they discussed whether the French bread had had too much garlic in it, and Lucy said that Mary Blake was really very goodhearted, only a little dull, and wasn't Harp a dear to go off down to bed without a protest? But they were both thinking about another conversation faintly heard beneath their talk.

"Where's Dad, Mother?" Rich came into the kitchen to ask, and Lucy stooped to scowling at him in quick telegraphic language. "He and Uncle Jim are talking, dear. I wouldn't disturb them now."

Rich hesitated. "Oh, well, g'night," he said, and went back upstairs.

"Isn't it wonderful that they've always been so close all these years?" Lucy said. But she couldn't hear what Phyllis answered because she was wiping silver and it clattered as she laid it in the drawer.

They finished the dishes, and Lucy went into the dining room to put the milk glass in the corner cupboard. Through the long windows, she could see the men out on the flagstones. James was sitting at the table and Josh was facing him, one foot on the bench. His voice came clearly through the open windows.

"Jim, let's get this straight. You believed in the boy and he let you down. You said yourself that he got mixed up with a girl and let his work go and then he flunked his exam and got panicked. This kind of thing happens every day, only the boy merely flunks out and he doesn't commit suicide. I don't for the life of me see why you insist on crucifying yourself over it."

Lucy put the last goblet in the cupboard so carelessly it clinked against the others, but she closed the door without looking to see whether it was nicked. Josh was letting his impatience get into his voice the way he did with Rich.

Phyllis came in from the kitchen, hesitating an instant in the doorway, and the light caught her there in her white dress with a scarf knotted at her neck. The scarf was blue, a dark cobalt blue . . .

"Have you worn that color before, Phyl?" Lucy asked.

"Oh yes. I wear it too much, I'm afraid. I'm so light, you know. Why?" Phyllis asked.

"It's becoming," Lucy murmured. "I have that color on the loom," she added with reluctance. But Phyllis was hardly listening.

"I think I'll run on down to the house, Lucy. Thank you. It was a very nice party."

"I've known better," Lucy said. "I was sick about Tom's saying that to Jim, but anyway, it's so good for Jim to talk to Josh."

"Yes," Phyllis said softly, looking through the window at the men. "I've been hoping he would without Josh having to ask him."

"I'll walk down with you," Lucy said. They went together across the flagstones and down the steps. Josh called out good night, and James said, "I'll be down in a few minutes." Then they went on talking, the tenseness of their voices carrying their words out to the women. Instinctively, Lucy and Phyllis were silent.

"Just let me tell you this, Josh," James was saying. "I thought about the boy's having the brains to go ahead in physics, maybe win the biggest scholarship anyone won in the whole city of Chicago and that was all I thought about. I coached him and gave him extra work and had him over at the house night after night. I never stopped to think about his own life. He came from a poor family; his father had a little cleaning and pressing place. I even took him up to the lake and got him a job at a camp so he would study evenings. Your friend was quite right tonight about exerting pressure."

Lucy and Phyllis were standing still in the path. Lucy felt Phyllis catch her breath, and she reached out and touched her arm, but Phyllis gave no sign of response.

"So what?" Josh interrupted.

"So what! Can't you see I did it because my own pride was wrapped up with this? Maybe I thought this would prove to myself that I was doing a great job teaching in Bellevue. I've always known you felt I should go on from there, that I should get into the kind of work I used to talk about doing, or teach in college, where I could do some research. Oh, I didn't put it into words, but, underneath, I had the feeling that Leonard's success would show you . . . anybody . . . that I wasn't wasting my time. I was just using him, without knowing it, to build up my own self-esteem. Once, when he seemed tired of working so steadily, I told him he . . . he couldn't let me down. Now do you see why I feel responsible for his death?"

The question hung motionless in the July night. Phyllis covered her face with her hands and sat down on the edge of the steps.

"Jim, for Christ's sake, you're a damned neurotic over this. Of course I don't see any such thing. You're simply letting this get away from you."

36

James's voice was so quiet and colorless that Lucy winced. "No. I don't think so, but I have to face it."

"The boy's dead. You can't help him now, and I can't be any help to you if you hug this guilt complex you've dreamed up. You've got to put it out of your mind and forget about it."

Lucy stirred restlessly. Josh was too vehement, too impatient.

"I shan't forget it very soon," James said.

"Phyl, it's good for him to say it, to get it out," Lucy whispered.

"Yes. I'm glad of that," Phyllis said. She lifted her head, but it was too dark to see her face. "Don't you see, he doesn't listen to what Josh says. Josh can't reach him either."

"He will, though. The summer will do a lot for him. Don't worry, Phyl." Lucy felt inadequate murmuring things she wasn't sure of herself. Still, it was true; Josh would make him see. For an instant, Lucy wanted to kiss Phyllis as she would Ellie, but Phyllis stood too stiffly, her face carefully turned away from the path of light. Lucy had a feeling that she wanted her to go, so she said, "Good night, Phyllis."

Phyllis was relieved that Lucy did not offer to come any farther with her. Instead of going in just yet, she sat down on the stone wall, beyond the path of light from the big house. Alone in the dark without anyone to see her, she could go back over what James had said. Hearing him say those things aloud gave her a hopeless feeling. He wasn't over it at all.

And he was so wrong. How could he think he had helped that boy because of his own pride? He had been excited that the boy was so bright. "I've got a real wizard in physics at last, Phyl; smart as a whip!" She remembered the day at the beginning of school when he came home and told her that. "I've got to see what I can do for him when the time comes," he had said. Didn't he remember?

And what kind of a pressure had he exerted? Those few

times when the boy stayed late, James had said he better spend the night, he lived so far away. She remembered the first time she made up the couch in the study for him, his quick, dark-eyed smile and his saying, "Jees, Missus Cutler, thanks. That's swell." There had been no pressure, only kindness.

She had carefully not told James what the boy's father had said that day about his feeling he had to do whatever James said. But perhaps the poor man had told James himself.

She moved her fingers over the stone beside her, feeling the clinging velvet moss and the lichen, which crumbled as she touched it and left the granite rock underneath rough and bumpy, so different from the smoothness of the marble benches in the library.

The light went off downstairs in the house, and the path across the orchard disappeared as though a strip of carpet had been rolled up. There was only one light, high under the gabled roof. A branch threw a shadow against the clapboards. James would be coming now. She would stay here until he came and he would know she had been waiting for him.

She listened so hard for the first sound of his feet on the grass that she heard a feathery jostling in the tree by the wall. The light under the gable went out, and the branch was lost against the darkness of the house. The sky seemed lighter.

This was the way she had waited so many times on the steps of the apartment house after her father left them, not really waited, because she knew he wasn't coming back, but not wanting to go in to her mother's dull-eyed look and always a record playing and the loneliness of their four rooms. She had almost forgotten this feeling that belonged to the years before she met James. She had thought it would never come again. But here it was. Not the same; twisted into something different, but still the same fear of separation, of loss. You were never safe; she had always known it.

The flat stone rocked against the next one as she stood up

and went back across the orchard. Maybe Josh and James were still talking outside. But there was no sound of voices. She went up the steps noiselessly and stood on the flagstones close to the sleeping house. Lucy would be lying so safely with Josh. There was nothing they could do to help James after all.

Maybe James had gone down the driveway to the road. But when she came to the end of the drive, the road was empty. Maybe he was back at their house by now. She hurried back up the drive, past the house, without looking at it, and through the wet grass of the orchard, not bothering to keep to the path. James wasn't there when she let herself in. She wished he had come and not found her so he would have gone hunting her, calling through the dark. Nobody called her name the way he did.

It was close in the low-ceilinged room. The shade on the old milk-can lamp was crooked, and she straightened it and left one bulb burning. Harp was asleep across his bed, his pillow, as usual, on the floor. So she covered him up and put his pillow on the chair.

She was still awake when she heard James come in.

"James? I've been so worried. Where have you been?" That wasn't what she had meant to say at all.

"I took a walk after Josh went in. It's only a little after midnight."

"I tried to find you. I walked way down the road."

"I'm sorry. I went the other way, toward the mountain. I always go there when I want to walk."

"Show me where it is tomorrow."

"I will," he said, but she felt that he was too far away for her to reach.

Six

WHEN LUCY saw Josh working on the stone wall the next morning, she knew he was upset. He always had to do something with his hands when things bothered him; that was why the farm was good for him. At home, he made clay masks of Caesar and Homer and Plato, laying them out on a board placed across the laundry tubs, with a wet cloth over them. Invariably, he was disappointed in them, and if they cracked, as they sometimes did when they were baked in a kiln, he was personally aggrieved. But if they turned out well, he carried them to college and set them on the top of the long bookcase in his office, taking a diffident pleasure in the effect they had on students who came in for conferences.

Working in the garden here at the farm or shingling a roof or rebuilding the old walls was better for him; the results were always admirable. He needed visible achievements the more, she sometimes felt, because he had to wait so long to see the achievements of his teaching take human form. He would have been as upset as James over that boy if he had been his student, but he wouldn't take it the way James was doing. He would be disappointed and disturbed in his own failure in judgment, but he wouldn't blame himself for urging the boy to do something he wasn't suited for. Then she wondered why she was so sure of that. He was just as sensitive . . . but he was different from Jim. She liked to listen to him directing the boys.

"Now look for a flat one, Harp, as big as this one, and have it all picked out. All right, Rich, you take the crowbar and work it under here while I lift."

Lucy peeled the sheets off the bed and bundled them up

to take down to wash, but she stood a minute longer by the window. She had a sudden sharp sense that she would always hold the sight of Josh and the boys in her mind, just like this, Josh with that old blue shirt, looking like some early New Englander building his walls. He had such strength and he took satisfaction in using it. She liked the granite rock in his hands as he stood off to look at the wall.

"We need to make it a stone higher all along, Harp."

"Where you going to get the stones, Uncle Josh?"

"Oh, we'll find them, Harp. Plenty of stones in this country. But this one won't do." When he dropped the boulder on the ground, it gave a dull sound that seemed to her to plumb the solid strength of the earth. The ground here might be crabbed and worn out, as people were always saying. Maybe the soil was thin, but it was firm under you. Lucy felt a sudden tenderness for it, thistles and stones and wild mustard and fireweed, that flag of an exhausted soil . . . all of it. Then her mind came back to Josh.

He was troubled about Jim, of course, and upset by what Jim had said about his chapters. That was why he had set to work on the wall instead of going to his study first. "I'm going to work every morning until noon, Lucy, until I get the damned thing done," he had said when they came.

Lucy made up the bed fresh, pulling the sun-dried sheets tight and making them firm at the corners. Wonderful to have to have a blanket here in the summer. In the city, they would be sweltering. The old blue Morning Star spread her grandmother had woven always pleased her. It had been made big enough to tuck under the pillows and hang down over the side rails, and the pattern was perfect; not a mistake anywhere. It would belong to Ellie some day, heritage of an ordered and ample way of life. After she finished the cloth on the loom, she would start one like this for Rich. She thought she had learned how to do it now, but she wanted to start such a big thing when she wasn't going to be interrupted so much. If it weren't for Josh, she might not invite anyone some summer. Have long uninterrupted days to sit at her loom and weave. She might snatch an hour right now while the clothes were washing. Josh and the boys were busy, and Ellie had gone over to see Jim and Phyl.

But she had sent the shuttle back and forth no more than half a dozen times when Josh appeared at the lattice.

"The wall's going to look fine across there," she said.

Josh grunted. "Lot to do on it. The boys are tired out so I told them we'd stop for today and go fishing if we can get Jim to go."

She let the rhythmic sound of the loom as she beat the cloth take the place of talk. She could hear the washing machine, too, but far off behind closed doors.

"Have you seen Phyl this morning?" Josh asked.

"Not yet. I hoped they might have slept late. I let Ellie take some blueberries over for their breakfast. Do get Jim to go off fishing; that's what he needs."

As Josh went across the shed, his long shadow fell heavily on the loom. He brought back one of the empty spools the thread came on and began whittling it to a point as he sat in the open door.

"I knew he was depressed, but I thought Phyl was exaggerating the other night."

"I'm sure she wasn't."

"No. In fact, I hope she didn't hear too much of what Jim was saying. He's got a regular obsession about how everything he did for the boy was because of his own pride, because he wanted to prove that teaching there in that high school was the most important thing he could do with his life. Now he feels guilty because he thinks he forced this boy to do what he wanted him to do. I told him he was going to ruin Harp's life and Phyl's, too, if he kept on this way. He seemed to register a little on that, finally."

Lucy listened to the sound of the loom and the thin slap of the scallops that shot off from Josh's knife. There was no point in telling Josh how much Phyllis had heard.

"I don't understand it, Lucy. Jim's always been so sensible and clear-headed."

"I know," she said, and then she saw the mistake in the weaving. The last three rows would have to come out. Now that there was more of it, the cobalt blue looked garish, but

42

she had gone too far to take it all out. "Do you think he should see someone, Josh, I mean a psychiatrist?"

"Good God, no!" Josh threw the spool across the grass, where it took down a blue spire of delphinium as it struck. "We don't want to suggest that the thing is that serious. He thinks he's just facing the truth about himself that he's never seen before. We've got to help him get straightened out, that's all."

After a moment, Lucy said, "You can, Josh, if anyone can. But it isn't going to be a restful summer for you the way I hoped it would."

"I don't need a restful summer. Good Heavens!" he burst out so loudly she was afraid someone would hear him, "If we can help Jim, that's all I care about."

He went over to the wall and got another spool and sat down again in the doorway, but he held it in his hands without whittling. The monotonous sound of the loom was soothing to her; maybe Josh felt it, too. But when he spoke, his voice was so low she held her hands still.

"Jim's such a tender fellow, you know, that boy's death's just torn him apart."

She turned on the bench so she could see him. Josh's face was grave. He was looking down and the strong line of his profile was cut against the open doorway. Josh was another, she thought. So devoted to Jim he could be torn apart, too.

Josh got up and started toward the house. Then he came back again. "Lucy"—this time he was smiling broadly —"while Jim's here, I'm going to get him to help me cut out some of those trees so we can have a better view from the house. They're closing in on us."

"Good idea," she said, smiling back at him, and went on with her weaving.

"What's Aunt Phyllis doing?" she asked when Ellie appeared.

"She's sitting out in the orchard reading, and she said for me to tell her when it's convenient and she'll come up and use the washing machine."

43

"She can have it now, only I think she better wait till after lunch." Suddenly, she didn't want the sound of the machine, barely within ear's reach but still there, beginning again. But, of course, she had said "Use it any time." The last time, Phyllis had washed everything in the big straw hamper along with her own things.

"Gracious, you didn't need to do that!" she had said to Phyllis, minding a little. But Phyllis insisted that she felt like it, that it was easier to be busy sometimes.

She had known what Phyllis meant, of course. But she had never seen a person who could sit so idly with her hands quiet in her lap. "Why don't you try weaving?" she had suggested. "Oh, I'd only mess it up," Phyllis had said. And secretly Lucy was relieved. Sometimes Ellie or Josh tried weaving a few inches, but usually she had to take it out later.

Phyllis was never in the way, and yet Lucy was aware of her all the time. Mary Blake had stopped her in the village the day after the party and asked about Phyl. "Who is she? She says so little and yet you keep wondering about her. Tom said she was so tense she made him nervous. I don't see that, do you? She's rather quiet and pale, don't you think?" But, yes, she did know what Tom meant.

Lucy thought back again to Jim's first letter about her. "I've found the girl," he had written. It was toward the end of the war, when he was stationed near Chicago. Phyllis's mother had died, and they had decided to be married at once, she remembered. Josh had fumed because as soon as Jim got out of the army he had taken a job teaching in high school and given up all his plans for research.

She and Josh were on their way to California when they finally met Phyllis, and they didn't see her long enough to get more than an impression. She had been surprised to have Phyllis look so young. "Nice enough," Josh had said, "but not the one I'd have expected James R. to pick out, would you?" Lucy remembered the other thing Josh had said, so resentfully she had teased him about it. He had said "Jim looks at her as though she were the princess of the fairy tale, all right." They had pieced together some slight picture of her background from what Jim had said to Josh, and wished Jim and Phyllis were not so hard up financially. Her mother and father had been divorced, and Phyllis had very little.

They always liked her notes on the Christmas card Jim wrote. Usually, she commented on some nonsensical remark of Jim's, or added a sentence that made a picture of their life. She remembered one: "We sat down purposefully to write Christmas cards, but we will get nowhere at all because James insists on stopping to reminisce about you both. Some Christmas James says we must all be in Vermont together. I should love it." "Why doesn't she ever call him Jim?" Josh wondered. They had always talked about the four of them getting together up here some Christmas and what a riot it would be. Well, here they were now, only it was summer.

Lucy ran the dark-blue thread through again, letting it lie heavily against the light green. But they ought to have a wonderful time. That was what Jim needed, and Phyllis, poor child. She got up abruptly and pulled the dustcloth over the loom. Then she hunted up Ellie.

"Since Dad and Uncle Jim and the boys are going off fishing, ask Aunt Phyllis to come up and have lunch with us."

Seven

WHEN PHYLLIS FINISHED hanging up the clothes, Lucy was still at her loom, so she could leave without explaining or pretending to be casual. Not that she had to do either, yet she felt self-conscious. They had had a good time at lunch, but she had felt Lucy trying to be lively, as though she wanted to get her mind away from James. Josh must have talked to her about him last night. She hated that, yet why should she? They had come so that Josh could help them. But to have someone, even Josh, talk about James just now bothered her. It seemed to separate her a little farther from him. Sometimes in the middle of the day, out in this sunny place, she felt there was nothing to worry about. He'd be all right. Then some expression on James's face, his sitting with a book but not reading it, would make her aware that he had retreated again into that place in his mind where he didn't take her.

Everything good had begun with James; everything gay and silly and sure. The night they had danced at the amusement park, a stranger had looked at them and smiled, and James had told her that everyone who looked at her loved her. She had laughed at the absurdity of it. People had never much looked at her at all, but when he said it, she almost believed it for a moment.

It was the Ugly Duckling story, she had told James. They had a joke about it, and in the copy of Hans Christian Andersen's fairy tales he gave her he had written, "To my lovely long-necked Swan." But he hadn't called her his swan for a long time.

She didn't want to go in the house, so she crossed the orchard and climbed the stone wall on the other side and

46

followed the faint grassy ruts that led up the hill. Harp had said there was an old cellar hole here somewhere. "The Engle place," James had said it was. She would have gone by without seeing it except for the doorstep with a sprawling old lilac bush on one side and a feeble pink rose-bush that seemed to lean against the wall that wasn't there. Still, when she stepped on the flat stone with the hollow worn in it, she felt as though she stood in front of a door. Too bad the cellar hole was choked with weeds. If she were a child, she would like to clean it out and play house down there. As it was, she played a moment, looking to see what the woman who had lived there had known from her door-way: the same mountain, that field, even this tree. And she followed what must have been the path to the road that went past the house. Perhaps there would be a neighbor's cellar hole beyond. But, instead, the road brought her without warning to an iron gate between two tipsy stone posts that led into a cemetery.

She had had enough of death, thank you. She and James had gone to that boy's funeral, and James had sat through it looking as white as that marble monument. She hadn't been able to think about the boy, not even to care about him, only about James.

But this small field with the crooked slate headstones was not like any cemetery in the city, bristling with monu-ments that resembled ugly Victorian buildings. The writing on the slate was not cut so deeply as names chiseled into granite or marble; it was more like writing on a school blackboard. She went in just to read the names. Quaint names they were, too quaint to stand for people you knew: Abigail, Jepsabah, Ephraim. And the flowery poems in which loss and moss rhymed together, and love and dove, and life and strife, hardly touched her more than old lace valentines. Over and over was repeated the last solemn warning, as though people couldn't think of anything else to put on a gravestone,

> Tread softly here . . .
> As you are now, so once was I

47

As I am now so you will be
Prepare to die and follow me.

But it was only some bitter New Englander getting a chance to frighten his children and neighbors. The person whose bones lay beneath the stone would never have said that. And what of it, anyway? It was the deaths that happened while you were treading softly here that mattered. The good bright sun was so warm that she took off her sweater in satisfaction with the heat.

The sun drew out the smell of pine trees by the wall and some sweet scent of fern or maybe honeysuckle. Wasn't that little pink flower on that half-dead bush honeysuckle? James would know. She liked the loud brassy yellow of the golden glow over in the corner of the wall. It was like the loud blare of a trumpet in this quiet place.

The earliest date she found was 1789; 1850, 1804 . . . these deaths had come too long ago to hurt now. No wonder people always went to old Vermont cemeteries. It was restful to know that all the people who had mourned were gone and all their grief had come to an end and been forgotten. You could only feel rather gentle about them, not sad.

She had to kneel down to read the next one. The slate stone was smaller, but shaped like the taller ones, just the head cut out of the rectangle of slate, the way you cut paper dolls from a folded sheet of paper.

AMANDA, AG. 4 YRS. 3 MOS.

Child of Danger, nursling of the storm
Sad were the woes that wrecked thy lovely form
No winds or rocks can shelter or delay
Thy sleep, since thy home is far away.

Wasn't every child a child of Danger, a nursling of the storm? Wasn't Harp, and James, and she herself?

She moved across the vague green aisle to the next one.

WILLIAM, DROWNED 1841, AG. 18.

The sea was a long way from this green valley. Why had William gone to sea? There was no war then. Maybe he had run away to find a white whale for himself.

"Boy, the white whale found you!" she said aloud, feeling strong in her flippancy. "But . . . maybe he didn't go to sea. That boy was eighteen. Maybe he . . . had . . . drowned himself. . . ." Her voice broke unexpectedly. The sound was a sacrilege in that grief-transmuted acre. She stood outside herself and heard it, and the choked sob that followed it, then she squeezed between the gate and the post and fled down the grass-rutted road.

When she came through the orchard she saw Lucy.

"I've been looking for you. The boys came back from fishing and are down at the old Quarry, swimming. Put on your bathing suit, and I'll be out in front."

When Phyllis climbed into the jeep, she said, "Thanks for coming back for me."

Lucy glanced at her quickly. "I almost didn't. I thought maybe you would like to get away by yourself for a little. There are times when I want to be left alone myself." Her sentences came out as a question.

"No, I'd been alone long enough," Phyllis said. "I went up an old road that goes past a cemetery."

"That's a lovely old cemetery they don't use any more. I like to go there. Peace always comes dropping slow."

"Because they don't use it any more," Phyllis said.

"Same way with old cellar holes and abandoned farms around here. Josh and I like to prowl them."

"But I think I prefer to go to a place that is free from old living, absolutely clear of joy or grief or anyone's hopes or fears."

"No," Lucy said slowly. "There's a kind of strength in a pattern made of other lives."

What were they really saying to each other, Phyllis wondered. Somehow they were explaining deep differences in themselves, without quite understanding them. They hadn't said as much before.

In another voice, Lucy said, "I think James had a good time fishing. He got some beauties."

Lucy was saying that to cheer her. Phyllis wondered if her eyes showed that she had been crying.

The black-brown water of the quarry was different from the chlorine blue of swimming pools, where you could see the safe tile bottom, or the water of Lake Michigan, where ripples grew to waves and waves subsided once again to quiet water. This was brooding and impenetrable, catching the light only to drown it in hidden depths. The shouting of the children, the splash as Harp did a belly flop, the floating rubber raft seemed incongruous in this place in the woods. It was too remote and eerie. A great rock rose seven or eight feet at one side, and at the top a tree bent over it. Moss-covered rocks walled the pool, and there was no outlet.

Her eyes could not find James at once, then she saw him swimming under water.

"Look at that boy!" Josh called to her. "He could always swim under water longer than anybody else."

She hung over the edge watching. The movement of his limbs made a strange slow flash of white in the opaque depths. He seemed unreal, separated from her by this dark near-stagnant water, moving deeper, farther away.

"This is the best place to get in; there's no beach," Lucy called. "That's the worst of it, you have to just dive in." She and Josh were on the side where the sun warmed the rocks, and Ellie bobbed up and down, clinging to the raft. But James was at the far end, where the high rock deepened the shadowed surface.

Hardly knowing what she called back, nor that she told Harp to be careful dear, nor that the water felt heavy and cold, she dropped off the edge and swam after James. Once, she dropped her legs and pulled them up again in fear at the sensation of endless depths. The temperature of the water changed. Now it was sluggishly warm to her face and shoulders but cold clutched at her legs, something tangled and slimy brushed her arm, and her hand caught at mud that oozed between her fingers. Her heart pounded and she couldn't see James. She kept her eyes on the tree and the edge of the water, swimming for herself now, to get out in safety. Then she saw him there ahead of her, shaking the water out of his face.

"Hi! Lucy found you." He pulled himself up against the rocky bank and gave her his strong, cold hand so she could climb out. "Doesn't this Quarry hole make a fine swimming pool?"

"Great!" She laughed because he was there and safe and real. How crazy that the water had seemed malevolent or that she had been so frightened.

"It's warmer in the water," she said and slid in again, floating a moment before she swam back to him, feeling herself moving in a stately fashion on the polished surface. Now she could see the shadow of her face and neck in the dark mirror . . . like a swan. If he would only see and call her that. "Look, James!" Her body was light and free and deliciously cold. She felt her hair running wet. But she couldn't wait for him to say it, for fear he had forgotten.

"I feel like a swan," she said, lifting her head out of the water, smiling.

Josh swam up to them with powerful strokes.

"See my swan?" James said.

"Looks more like a mermaid to me," Josh said. "Look at mine, floating on a raft."

Eight

"YOU THINK it's all right to go off like this and leave them?" Lucy asked, fastening the braid around her head. "Tom and Mary are having this party just for them, of course, but Phyllis said Jim didn't feel up to it. I didn't want to push it."

Josh pulled a clean shirt gingerly over his fresh tan. "Of course it's all right. We can't cut our cloth entirely to his pattern. I told Jim he must make an effort to get out. Phyllis ought to insist on it."

Lucy's face sobered. "It's awfully hard on her, Josh. She looked as though she had been crying yesterday. She'd been up to the old cemetery."

Josh tied his tie, looking over Lucy's head in the mirror. "I'm sure it is. Jim's changed so I can hardly believe it's Jim. If there was anybody I would have said could take anything, it was Jim."

"He was fine, though, at the swimming pool. Give him time; the whole thing is too fresh in his mind." Josh was getting upset. "Phyllis offered to get supper for Rich and Ellie, too, so they're all going to eat up here."

"That's fair enough," Josh said.

Jim was out on the flagstones playing chess with Rich when they came down. Ellie was hanging over the arm of his chair. Harp was watching the charcoal grill, and Phyllis was busy in the kitchen. Lucy could see Josh wishing he were not going out.

"Well, you look right smart for an elderly professor!" Jim razzed. Lucy was relieved to hear the playful tone of voice. He looked relaxed and at ease. She would point this out to Josh on their way, but why couldn't Jim go with them? He was trying.

"And you have all the smug satisfaction of a middle-aged businessman home from the office, you sloth, you!" Josh retorted. "But you're smoking like a house afire. Tell you, the way I stopped smoking was to carry something in my pocket. I carried an 06 shell and every time I itched for a cigarette I reached in my pocket and fingered it. Take something . . . here, take this agate. It'll give you something to have in your hand." He tossed the black-and-amber agate over to Jim. "Rich gave it to me, but if it helps you stop smoking, it's in a good cause. That all right, Rich?"

Rich looked up from the chessboard. "Sure, if you don't hold up our game any longer."

"I don't promise anything. I don't even know that I want to stop smoking," James said, slipping the agate into his pocket.

"You're good to feed Ellie and Rich, Phyllis," Lucy said. It gave her an odd feeling to see Phyllis there in the kitchen. They had thought her so thin and pale and rather unsure that time Jim brought her to meet them. She could see as she looked at Phyl standing there by the window in that green dress what he must have seen in her.

"I enjoy doing it," Phyllis said. "Have a good time and don't give us a thought. We've been so much on your minds."

She said it almost as though she resented their helping, didn't she? Lucy wondered, but she went on without trying to answer beyond saying thank you. Rich was too absorbed in his game to look up, and Ellie called out, "Can we use the big hurricane lamps, Mother? We're going to sit late around the table." Lucy was ashamed of the twinge she felt at seeing someone else in their places.

Phyllis hunted for another bowl for salad. Lucy always used the big red one. On an impulse she took down the pottery after-dinner coffee cups with a sense of pleasure.

But halfway between the cupboard and the table, the pleasure went flat. These were Lucy's things, this was Lucy's house. The very kitchen seemed a symbol of Josh's and Lucy's secure living; their own rented house in Illinois was far away and the little kitchen over in the guesthouse across the meadow was as unreal as their lives were now, a temporary makeshift. A great wave of homesickness washed up over her mind. They might be by themselves and "as independent as calves in clover" but they were dependent on Josh's and Lucy's kindness. Josh and Lucy were wonderful and generous and concerned . . . they did everything to make them feel welcome, but tonight she had felt she and James were a burden to them.

Still, Josh had said, "If Lucy was worried about me, I'd expect her to go to Jim." But didn't he think, really, that such a thing could never be? He was sure that he himself would never go to pieces. She set the little cups down on their saucers, one by one. She didn't believe Joshua Blair would.

James had intended going to the Blakes' tonight. And then, just before time to dress, he had said, "I'm sorry, but I can't do it, Phyl. You go." She looked out the window across the fields to the wooded mountain, dark green now in the late light. The color was falling out of the sky, leaving only dullness behind.

"They're done, Mom. The hamburgers are done," Harp called.

"All right. Ellie, you come and get the plates." But she stood still a moment longer. Harp had said today, "Let's stay here, Mom. Nobody knows about Dad and that boy here."

James was waiting for Rich to make the next move, sitting back in his chair with that closed, withdrawn look.

"James," she said almost sharply, "can you and Rich come now?"

Nine

LUCY WENT OUT to talk to Josh by the wall. He had
been working steadily all morning, making the boys work,
too. Now they had gone for the mail, and Josh called to her
to come and bring some coffee.

"I thought Jim was going to help you with the wall?"

Josh shrugged. "I haven't seen him this morning. I talked
to him about a job at the Perkins-Elmer Labs. You know,
Lucy, the more I think of it, the more desirable that seems."

Lucy could see that in Josh's mind the place was already
available, offered to Jim on a platter. "Was Jim interested?" she asked.

"Oh, he said he wouldn't have a chance at it; all his experience was in teaching and he didn't have enough training."

In a way, she was relieved that Jim realized this was still
in Josh's mind. "What about that?"

"I'm going to get Hopkins over here. He's always on the
lookout for a good man, and Jim's no slouch, you know. He
could get plenty of good recommendations. Why, Jim was
twice as bright as most of us in college."

She liked Josh's saying that. It was like him.

"If Jim hadn't gone off and married Phyllis when he did,
he'd have one of the top jobs in some place like that by
now."

"Don't let Phyllis know you think that, Josh. That
would hurt her, particularly now."

"I don't intend to, but it's true. I don't suppose she had
any conception of what was important to James's career."
Josh rolled the crowbar back and forth under his foot. "I
called Hopkins up. He sounded interested right away."

55

How fast Josh worked. It would be hard not to be interested in a person Josh believed in. "What will you do, take Jim over to see him?"

Josh rolled the crowbar so hard it hit the flagstones with a clatter. "Jim said he had to have a little while to think things out. But then he said perhaps he shouldn't go on teaching. Maybe he wasn't fit to. I get out of patience with that dramatizing he does."

"Oh, Josh . . ."

"Well, maybe not that, but the way he insists on feeling guilty."

Lucy saw Jim and Phyllis coming across the meadow. "Good morning!" she called. "But if he does, I don't believe he can help it, Josh," she said in a low voice.

"You two have done a day's work while we've been idling," Phyllis said.

"Here, boy!" Josh shoved the crowbar across the grass to Jim.

"Thanks," Jim said with a grin. "Lucy, doesn't this make you think of the time Josh told your father he'd redo the tennis court and then after he'd got the credit for that magnificent gesture, he came around and expected you and the Dunlap girl . . . what was her name? Kitty, Kitty Dunlap, and me to work with him?"

Lucy laughed. "Exactly. And Kitty kept saying, 'But, Josh, you're so strenuous!' "

"Say, if I remember correctly, that little girl was smitten with James R.," Josh remarked. "I remember how you two read *Farewell to Arms* aloud," Josh went on. "You were the romantic, bookish type that summer, Cutler."

"Oh, that was a long time ago," Lucy interrupted. "Kitty's married and lives down in Nashville, I hear." All this reminiscing wasn't any good for Phyllis. This was what made her feel like an outsider.

Phyllis said, "*Farewell to Arms* is one of the books that goes out as fast as it comes in to the library. Always taken out by young people. When I was at the checking desk, I used to imagine that they brought it back sort of reverently, as though it had changed them."

"You have to be young to read that book," Josh said. "Anybody beyond the state of adolescence isn't going to believe that going AWOL is heroic."

"Frederick Henry didn't think of himself as particularly heroic, did he?" James said. "Wasn't it that he distrusted heroics?" He reached over to pull a long grass to suck.

"Maybe, but he's a lesser person on account of his actions."

"You know, Josh, you want life in explicit terms of black and white, good and bad" James said. "You just can't accept flaws in people. Your friends must be hard on you." But he didn't look at Josh. Instead, his eyes were watching the boys coming back up the road with the mail.

"Where've you been?" Lucy asked, glad of their coming just then. "You went ages ago." Then she saw Rich's face. He gave Josh a letter and the paper and dropped a letter on her lap. It bore the heading of the college on the corner of the envelope. Rich's grades, of course. But why had he brought them to her? She opened the envelope quietly, noticing that Josh was deep in his own letter. Jim was looking at the paper, and Phyl was talking to Harp. She felt Rich waiting and glanced up at him. "They aren't very good," he said in a low voice.

She saw the condition in physics at once, but she said, "Good, Rich, you did well in history. Dad will be pleased about classics. . . ." He put his finger on the word "condition." The small boyishness of the gesture touched her. "Well, you had some trouble with that at the beginning." She wondered again if Josh hadn't been wrong to let him go into college at sixteen.

"Oh, you got your grades," Josh said.

Rich took the slip over to him. She could see Josh's disappointment, but none of it showed in his voice.

"Well, Rich, that's tough. Maybe you and Jim should go into a huddle. Would you take him on, Jim? Rich has a condition in physics, but he can take a re-exam in the fall."

"We'll talk about it, eh, Rich?" Jim said, taking the decision away from Josh, giving it to Rich.

"I study but I just don't get it," Rich said. "Sure, I'd like to talk to you about it," he added.

"How lucky you're here, Jim," Lucy said as Rich went off.

Josh picked up his letter. "This is from Crofton asking if I'll have the . . ." he hesitated an instant . . . "my book ready by the end of the summer."

No one spoke until Phyllis said, "We'll feel we are interrupting you by our being here unless you do."

"Well, old Jim here has rather brought me to a stop. If he doesn't think it's worth writing, I certainly don't intend to finish it."

Josh shouldn't say a thing like that, Lucy thought. But, of course, he cared so much about what Jim said. She felt, rather than saw, that Jim was lighting a cigarette, and that Phyllis and Harp were leaving.

"Of course, the answer to that is that if it seems worth writing to you, then it is," Jim said finally. "I told you I was no judge just now."

"I'll take that into consideration when you tell me what you think, but I would like to have you read the rest of it before I go on."

"Bring it out," Jim said.

Josh got up at once and went in to get the manuscript. Lucy lifted her hands in a gesture of hopelessness. "I'm sorry, Jim. I know you don't want to read it, but you can see he has to know what you think." She forgot for a moment that Jim was the difficult one. "Josh has had these ideas for a long time and now he's trying to put them down." She hesitated, wanting to say, "If you don't think they're good, you must say so," but she said instead, "They've helped so many boys. And you've no idea how often he's asked to speak at other colleges. . . ."

"I can't say something to Josh that I don't think. Not after all he's doing for me this summer."

"Is he, Jim? Is it really good for you to be here? It's wonderful for us to have you, but I didn't know."

"You've no idea, Lucy. I told Phyl this morning I

58

thought I'd have gone out of my mind if I had stayed home this summer."

Lucy got up when Josh came back. "Don't tear each other's hair out by the roots," she warned in another tone. "I'm going to weave, and if there's any sign of warfare, I'll come straight out."

How fine that Jim felt that way. He was so quiet and depressed at times that it was hard to tell whether it was good for him here. His not going to the Blakes' the other night had annoyed her as much as it had Josh. Josh was impatient at his not making more of an effort, but maybe it was a strain for him to talk to people just now. Maybe all Jim needed was time and being here with Josh. Josh never understood that what people got from him was a sense of strength and affection; he thought it was what he said to them or could do for them.

From where she sat, she could look way out across the meadow to the mountain. Always, the strong green line against the sky rested her. She thought how it would look in the fall when the whole mountain was a pattern of reds and yellows, or in winter when it was a black smudge of charcoal against the sky. She always meant to come up alone for a week some fall, but of course she never would. Josh would be upset even though he told her to go ahead. A small, pleased smile caught at the corners of her mouth. She could hear the murmur of the men's voices and sank now into her own content.

"But, Josh, read it for yourself!" Jim's voice was raised. "What you want to say gets lost. This stuff about 'clean-cut thinking' and 'thought processes that lay hold of the eternal verities.' These are nothing but clichés, Josh! Here, listen to this: 'the dogged refusal to be cajoled, convinced, or corrupted' . . . you just got carried away by the alliteration. I suppose, if I were honest about it . . ."

Jim was speaking slowly and his voice was hard.

". . . that's exactly what I did to young Leonard Gilespie; I cajoled him into studying harder than he ever wanted to, and convinced him that he could do it, and, obviously, I was corrupting him out of his natural way of life or any integrity of his own."

Lucy held her hand on the beater without bringing it forward. She had never heard Jim sound like that. Josh must say something quickly.

"Don't be an ass, Jim," he muttered. "I know the style is wordy in places, but when you help me weed out the verbiage a bit, what do you think of the ideas?" Josh was ignoring Jim's remark.

"Can you separate them?" Jim asked. "But maybe it is good, since that string of oratory seems to have hit me."

The silence was so complete after that, that she went to the doorway. Josh had gone over to the stone he had left on the ground. As he laid it on top of the low wall, it grated harshly against the other stones and settled with a hollow sound. Jim just sat there. He lit another cigarette and drew the smoke down into his lungs. When he did speak, his voice was quiet.

"I realize that one of the reasons you wanted me to read these chapters, Josh, is because you felt some of the things in here would be good for me. You feel that everything can be handled by sheer willing to do it."

Josh came back and sat down on the ground. "Yes, I do. I might as well say it. Barring illness or death, yes. The trouble with you is that you're letting this experience overwhelm you. You're not making any real effort to set it aside and go on. Yet the way you're going, as I told you the other night, is going to ruin your own and Phyl's life. And it's certainly having an effect on Harp's. Yesterday, when we were going over to the mill, I told Harp to see if you wanted to go. He just said, 'Dad won't want to go.' And look at your smoking. You were going to stop that, but you go right on."

Jim threw his cigarette away, but he said, "It's not quite as easy as all that, Josh." His voice was so low Lucy missed the last words, but she felt them. She banged the lattice door behind her.

"I thought we could all have lunch out here," she said.

Jim seemed relieved, she thought, for he stood up quickly. "Thanks, Lucy," he said. "I'll go see where Phyllis is."

They sat watching Jim go across the meadow. Josh's face was stern, his mouth tight, with little pockets at either jowl; he seemed to be studying the wall. Then he went over to the tumbled heap of stones and began to lay them in place. The work went faster alone than with the boys.

Lucy said, "Be patient with him, Josh. He told me this morning that he thought he'd have gone crazy if he hadn't been coming here."

"Did he say that?" Josh's face gentled. He shook his head. "I wonder what Phyllis says to him about all this. She looks worried so much of the time; you know that could gnaw at a man."

"I'm sure she doesn't let him see any of that. She adores Jim."

"He can't help but see it. A lot depends on her attitude. I've got to talk to her. You know, Lucy, I keep thinking of Jim the way I knew him before and forgetting that his marrying Phyllis shows a different side of him."

She seized on the chance for a light touch. "You mean you never know a man, really, until he's married?"

"Not in the same way," Josh answered in perfect seriousness. "I'm inclined to think that he's an abstraction to you till then. You know what he thinks about things, how he'll react. After he's married, you begin to see him fully as another man."

"Why, Josh, how fantastic! Does that make you change your idea about him then?"

"I suppose eventually you do, when you come to know his wife. You know how different Phyllis is from the kind of girl we would have expected Jim to marry." Josh stopped to wipe his face. "Where's Rich? The minute I let him go, he was off to that old hot rod he's tinkering with."

"Don't call it a hot rod, Josh. It makes him sound like a hood or something. He just likes to work on cars the way you like this." It was hard to explain Rich to Josh, yet they were so much alike. "Ask him to help you," she suggested. "He probably thought Jim was out here with you."

"Rich! I need some brawn here," Josh bellowed.

As though she had known beforehand the way it would be, she watched Rich appear around the corner of the barn. Always he filled her eyes when he appeared suddenly. He was tall like Josh. His hands and wrists were greasy and he had a smutch of grease on his face.

"Can't just this minute, Dad. I've bolts and screws all over the place."

"You think you know what's wrong this time?"

"I'm not sure; I think so. Jim had an idea about it I thought I'd try."

"You don't want to trust his ideas about machinery. He's got theories but about as much mechanical skill as Ellie has. Ask him about the time he was going to fix the plumbing in the fraternity house."

Josh was grinning. But she noticed that Rich went back to his car.

Ten

THE MID-JULY MORNING, it seemed to Phyllis, came hot as steel fresh from some astronomic foundry. But here at the farm it was finely tempered by the clover-fragrant air and cold-running water from the brook. The least sound—Lucy's egg beater across the meadow, the scrape of the lid of the cookie jar Harp was rifling, and the idlest comment, Jim's exclamation when his shoelace broke— struck against the steel, but the morning seemed to hang waiting for some loud sound to ring a peal of alarm from its curve. Alarm against what? Phyllis lifted her head to listen to the brassy rasp of grasshoppers.

Ellie pushed open the door of the screened porch. She was carrying the cat, in spite of the heat.

"Hello," Phyllis said. "Come in. I'm completely lazy. I started reading and I haven't even washed my dishes." Why did she explain to a child why she was sitting like this?

Ellie dropped the cat, but she continued to stand in the doorway. Phyllis felt her glance, cool, curious. Mostly, children did not really look at older people to see what they were like. Did Ellie find her uninteresting or merely grown-up? A sudden sharp envy stung her mind. Ellie was so complete in herself, so free because she hadn't given herself to any other person. Her life didn't hang on someone else's.

The sun coming around the corner of the green-slatted shade seemed to rest on Ellie. She lifted her dark hair, which had come unbraided, and held it up on her head, turning an instant's grown-up profile.

"Uncle Jim's part way up the mountain. I waved to him, but he didn't see me. I even called to him."

Whenever Josh did anything, he took one of the children or Lucy with him. He announced the trip, and everyone caught the spirit of the expedition. James simply got up from his chair and without a word walked off across the garden and on up the hill. "Why don't you go up and meet him?" Phyllis suggested. "He'd like that."

"Would he?" Phyllis could see her thinking how she would suddenly appear and he would look surprised and say "hello." She had probably never thought about a man's mood. But she would learn even as Lucy and she had.

Ellie shook her head. "It's too hot to climb." But Phyllis saw Ellie looking up at the mountain as she walked back around the house. She put the book down and went outside. There was no sign of James. He had gone too far away for Ellie to catch up to him now. Ellie was wiser than she was; she didn't keep trying to go with him.

Then Josh appeared. "I came over to talk to you so I wouldn't have to do anything useful or energetic. Whew, it's hot. Let's go out in the orchard where there's a good thick shade."

"Is Lucy slave-driving you?" she asked.

"No, just my conscience." As they climbed over the wall into the orchard, he said, "This is another tumble-down wall I meant to build up last summer. I sunk so much time in that blamed book I'm trying to do, I guess, I didn't get to it."

James had been so critical of his book; was that what he had come to talk about? She said quickly, "Josh, I hope you won't mind James's comments. I think this . . . experience with that boy has been such a terrible thing for him that he's unsure of everything he used to be so sure of. Words in books especially."

Josh reached for a blade of grass and chewed at the sweet stem before he went on. "Yes," he said slowly. "I think you're right. He's made up his mind that he killed the boy."

"Killed!" The word banged against the day's hot steel and set off a hideous clamor in her mind.

"Of course, he's crazy!" The impatience, almost anger, in Josh's voice stopped the reverberations in mid-air. Then, in a milder tone he went on. "You know, Phyl, there isn't any man in the world I care so much about as I do Jim. Ever since about the middle of college, what's happened to him has mattered to me. We were as different as any two people could be, I suppose, but we always seemed to understand what we were each driving at. Took us a long time, often. I remember some of the fool arguments we had, bitter ones sometimes. The other morning when Jim was talking about my book, I thought, We're arguing about the same thing we've argued about before."

"How do you mean, Josh?" What was it about his tone of voice that embarrassed her a little? She looked up through the old gnarled apple tree, and noticed how the tiny green knobs had grown and were striped with red, but they weren't good to eat.

"Well, I always maintained and I still do, more than ever, that the trouble with people is that they won't commit themselves to a decision or a line of action."

He must talk this way to students, Phyllis thought. How splendid he must be for them.

"And Jim used to say that people weren't always sure enough of themselves, that they had doubts that kept them from committing themselves. But that isn't the way the thing works. People become what they shoot at. Now he thinks in this book that I'm laying too much stress on a man's will. You know as well as I do, Phyl, that Jim's got to will to put this unfortunate mess out of his head. In the last analysis, no one can help him until he does that."

He made it sound so simple. Josh didn't understand. "Josh, James won't put that boy's death out of his mind unless you can make him see that it wasn't his fault. Can't you tell him about boys you've known? Show him it wasn't due to his pride . . ." She had difficulty keeping her voice from sounding frantic. "He's the most unconceited person; he never worries about what people think of him. . . ." She felt hopeless. "I'm afraid he's going to go on feeling guilty the rest of his life." She said the last words in a low voice, grudgingly, but they resounded against the still morning.

Josh threw away the grass he had been chewing. "He's finished if he takes that attitude, and even more surely if you do. Don't let him talk about it. When you see him getting into one of those silent moods, think of something to do. And don't let him know that you're worried about him. The first thing, as I see it, is to get him out of that place."

In an instant, she saw Oak Street and the tree in front of their house with the wire guard around the trunk. She unlatched the door and went into the hall that was always a little dark until she pushed the button and the lamp touched it with warmth and caught the blue backs of James's set of Conrad on the shelf inside the living-room door. She hadn't thought of their not going back; she had only thought of getting James away for a while.

"I never felt good about Jim's being content with teaching there," Josh said. "I doubt if teaching is his forte, anyway."

She saw the front door of the high school, where she let James out if she drove him over, and the boys speaking to him as he went in.

"If I can get a good opening for him with Perkins-Elmer Labs, he could go into the sort of work he's interested in, the sort of thing he always meant to do when he got out of college. But you've got to do your part, Phyl. If necessary, you've got to tell him you won't go back to Illinois to live."

She tried to hear herself saying that to James. He wouldn't believe her. . . .

"A lot of his attitude toward this whole thing is going to depend on yours."

She felt for a moment that he looked at her almost accusingly. What did he mean about her attitude? "I try to act as though it was all over and past, Josh, and we don't speak of it, but it's there in James's mind." She didn't even call it by name. "You can see how he is," she implored. The sky through the branches of the trees blurred in the brazen heat. The leaves were leathery and artificial. She wished James would come back.

"It's hard to understand his reaction," Josh murmured, studying the trunk of the tree in front of him. With one finger, he stopped an ant crawling through the narrow bark alleyways and made it go around by another route. "He's always had so much insight. . . ."

Josh looked at her, and he was smiling. "Don't you worry, Phyl. Jim's going to get all over this. You'll see!" His smile and the sureness of his voice refocussed the sky so that it was clear and blue. Oh yes, James would get all over this. As Josh gave her a hand, she had the feeling of being lifted up from the shadow of the orchard into some place where a cool breeze blew.

"Harp looks like a man on business," Josh commented as Harp came out to them.

"I was hunting all over for you, Uncle Josh," Harp said. "Can I use your power saw?"

"Sure you can, Harp, but I'll go over with you and stand by while you use it. Do you know where it is?"

"It's up over the shed where Aunt Lucy weaves."

"What are you building?" Josh asked.

"A boat for the pond, and then I'm going to paint her. Rich says there's some red paint I can have. May I?"

Josh smiled at Phyllis. "Bet you can," he promised.

Eleven

"REAL, HONEST-TO-GOODNESS summertime,"
Josh said, as they sat on the porch.

Lucy said, "In winter I dream of nights like this."

Some quality of the July night, warm, still, and luminous,
slowed their voices, Phyllis thought, and lightened them at
the same time. Josh and Lucy might have been speaking
lines of poetry to each other.

"Think how hot it must be at home, Phyl," James added.

"Or, rather, don't think." Phyllis leaned her head back
against the chair, and watched the sparks from the bonfire
in the meadow burn out as they rose in the air.

"We ought to move out on the flagstones, but these ancient rockers are so comfortable," Lucy said. Hers tapped
out a serene rhythm against the boards as she rocked. James
and Josh rested their feet on the railing, and they had to
move when Ellie wanted to get by.

"Can't you go around, Ellie?" Josh grumbled.

"I want to ask Mother something. Mother, why can't I
just go down and see the boys?" she whispered noisily.

"Because they're big boys and they want to be by themselves," Lucy said firmly. "They're not doing anything,
Ellie; they're just talking." But the bonfire flared up as
new fuel was added, and a roar of laughter came from the
meadow.

"See, they are having fun. Can I just go for a minute?"
Ellie teased.

"Didn't you hear Mother say no?" Josh asked. "That's
enough."

"Ellie, look at those fireflies. I've never seen such whop-
pers," James interposed. "I'll get out there in the dark

and you see if you can tell which is a firefly and which is my cigarette. Don't look now until I get there."

"Oh, I'm a firefly, I'm a katydid . . ." Josh sang to him. "Come here, Ellie, and I'll cover your face until Uncle Jim gets hidden."

"It's too bad Harp is sick," Phyllis said. "James thinks he must have eaten some green apples. He wouldn't eat any supper and he didn't want me to stay with him, but I thought I'd go down in a little while."

Ellie lifted her head from her father's shoulder. "I went down to see him and he said to go away."

"All right," James called in a high squeaking voice.

"I can't tell the difference," Ellie squealed. "Oh, there you are, in the snowball bush, Uncle Jim."

"You have to catch me," James answered.

"Jim seems like himself tonight, doesn't he?" Lucy exclaimed. "I love hearing him out there playing with Ellie."

"Yes," Phyllis said, but she didn't feel this was James. This was James making an effort to play with Ellie. James was the silent person who had gone off by himself on the mountain this afternoon, or who sat quietly reading, only to throw the book from him and sit looking out the window, the person who had burrowed his head under her breasts last night and held her so closely it ceased to be love and became a kind of desperation.

"We actually used to play children's games here in the summer after we were in college," Lucy said.

"Your mother loved to sit here and watch us," Josh remembered.

"And now here we are watching our own children. It's almost Chekhovian, isn't it?" Lucy said.

"Well, you have your orchard," James put in, still panting from his chase with Ellie.

"But it isn't going to be cut down," Josh said. "Though I am going to cut a couple of trees down to get a better view from here."

"I wonder what Mother would have thought of Rich and his friends down there?" Lucy asked. "Honestly, that's the most absurd affair. Rich says they'll try to stay awake all

69

night around the fire. They have a kind of truth party and tell each other all their faults. Can you imagine anything worse!"

"Kind of an ordeal at the edge of manhood, like the young braves used to have, only this is a psychological one," Josh explained. "They get a lot of things off their chests about each other and they learn how to take it. A little rough, maybe, but no one person is singled out. They all have to stand it."

"Gruesome!" Phyllis said. "Some of them must get hurt whether they show it or not, and then remember those things all their lives."

"Oh, I don't know," Josh insisted. "I can see some point in it."

"They don't know anything about themselves yet, nor does anyone else. I have trouble enough facing myself now," James said.

James was saying . . . the tone of his voice and the meaning underneath his words made Phyllis's heart beat nervously.

"Ellie," Lucy began, "don't you think you better go to bed?"

"I must go down and see that Harp is all right," Phyllis said.

"I'll go down with you," James began, but Josh said, "Don't go yet, Jim. I want to talk to you."

Phyllis was glad to go by herself. It was a relief to get away. Josh hadn't said anything, but she could feel his impatience with James's smoking, and then James's saying what he had said. If James should be offered a position in that lab Josh was talking about . . . but perhaps Josh was too optimistic about it. "If necessary, you've got to tell him you won't go back to Illinois to live. A lot of his attitude is going to depend on yours," Josh had said. It seemed like a conspiracy, but Josh understood these things. He knew better than she did what was best for James.

When she let herself in the house, Harp called from his room.

"Dear, are you feeling better?" When he was sick, she could call him tender names and he didn't mind. She turned on the lamp in his room. "Why, Harp, you've been crying."

Harp sat up, digging at his red eyes with his hand. "Mom . . ."

"What happened, Harp?"

He dived, face down, into the pillow, and his words came out muffled. "I spilled the paint. . . ."

"What paint? Harp, sit up and tell me. It can't be so terrible as all that."

But when Harp got the story out, it seemed worse.

"Did you look at Aunt Lucy's weaving?"

Harp nodded. "The paint made a big place on it. I didn't mean to, Mom, and I wiped it up right away."

"Of course you didn't mean to, Harp, but you should have told her as soon as it happened. You weren't sick at all, Harp, were you? You just . . . felt so badly it made you sick?" Like James, her mind insisted.

With a sudden lunge, he flung himself closer to her and buried his face against her knee. "What will Aunt Lucy say, Mom?"

"I don't know. She'll feel terrible, Harp. Her weaving means a great deal to her."

"I know," Harp said miserably. "Ellie said she won't let any of them touch it unless she's there."

"Did you tell Ellie?"

"Ellie saw it."

When Harp was dressed, they went back across the orchard without speaking, but she squeezed Harp's arm as they reached the porch.

"Well, Harp, do you feel better?" Josh called out to him.

"Nope," Harp said. Then he went stiffly over to Lucy. "Aunt Lucy, can I see you, please?"

"What happened?" James asked.

"He spilled paint in the loft above the shed and it came down on Lucy's loom," Phyllis explained. Under Josh's whistle and James's sharp exclamation, she could hear the low voices in the kitchen. In a minute, Harp and Lucy would go out to see the damage. But instead, Lucy came back alone.

"Harp and Ellie are having a slice of watermelon. Would any of you like some?"

"Oh, Lucy, I'm so dreadfully sorry," Phyllis said. "Is it completely ruined?"

"I haven't looked yet. It can't be more than a strip or two. Poor child, he suffered so over the thing he could hardly tell me." She sat down on the porch and began to rock slowly. "Look, they've built up their fire again down there." But Phyllis heard the tone of her voice rather than her words. Was she angry? Her voice seemed thin and high.

"Could we go and see how bad the paint is?" Phyllis asked.

"No, let's not bother now." Lucy answered a little too quickly, Phyllis felt.

"You certainly are wonderful about it," James said.

"It's my fault, really, Lu," Josh said. "I told him he could paint his boat up there. Now I'll get that floor over the shed fixed; it's nothing but loose boards."

"That's unnecessary; nobody would ever think of painting up there again in a dozen years," Lucy said.

Ellie and Harp came out of the kitchen. They looked banded together, Phyllis thought: against the grownups, or something bigger, perhaps. Josh went over and turned on the post light for them. "Tough luck, Harp, old man, but don't worry about it. Your Aunt Lucy's forgiven you," he said.

"Good night, son," James called, but Harp made no answer and he did not look around at them.

Lucy called after them, "Harp, would you and Ellie like to take your sleeping bags out on the south side of the porch to sleep tonight?" After a moment's consultation, Ellie's voice came back. "Harp doesn't want to." She added, "It's too mosquitoey."

"He feels too bad to be polite, I'm afraid," Phyllis tried to explain. Why didn't Lucy go to see the damage Harp had done? How could she just sit there without knowing? But how good she was about it. The light in James's hand flared as he lit his cigarette. The silence was uneasy, or was she just imagining it?

"There's somebody coming up from the fire," Josh said. "That's a flashlight; that isn't any firefly."

"It must be Rich coming for the watermelon," Lucy said.

Now they could hear the regular pound of feet running up the hill, and Rich leaped over the stone wall. The light from the post lantern drained the color out of his face and made the sweat glisten. His eyes were bright, his mouth open as he caught his breath. Phyllis stared at his T shirt clinging damply to his thin shoulders like . . . like the boy's after he had bicycled across the city hot nights to study with James.

"You'd do for an Indian runner," Josh said. "How's the council fire?"

"Fine," Rich said, dispelling the illusion of similarity for Phyllis the minute he spoke. He shook his head back and ran his hand over his close-cut hair. She felt a kind of unhealthy excitement in him. Ellie had come back up and stood staring at him.

"Dad, can I take some beer down . . . you know, just one can around? All the guys are used to drinking; all but Bill and me are seventeen or eighteen."

"Oh, you don't need beer. You take some Cokes to them," Josh said. "We've got some in the cooler. Jim, come on and tell Rich about the beer bust we had freshman year."

"That watermelon is on the ice, you know," Lucy called after them as they went into the house.

When they were alone, Phyllis said, "Lucy, I'm so worried about the paint. Please let me see how bad it is."

"Oh, forget it, Phyllis. It doesn't matter at all; really it doesn't. . . . Well, come and see it if you're going to worry."

When she had turned the switch by the shed door, they saw that the thick dark stain lay six or seven inches across the cloth beam and trailed off in a thinner line that had dripped on the bench.

"It couldn't be much worse," Phyllis said, looking back at Lucy. "What can you do? Can you cut it out?"

Lucy stood staring at the loom, her head tipped a little to one side. She spoke slowly. "As a matter of fact, I haven't liked the colors very well. That blue is too harsh for the pastel shades; I think I'll just cut it off and begin a new pattern. Really, I don't mind too much, Phyl. One time I left the lattice open myself and a drenching rain came in and shrank what I had on the loom. I'm sorry I got so tense about the thing."

"You're wonderful about it, Lucy," Phyllis murmured. What else was there to say? But she could see that Lucy did mind. She would always remember their spoiling her weaving . . . Harp, that is.

"I'll go on down, Lucy," Phyllis said. "I think James will want to stay a while."

"Oh yes, don't take Jim away yet. Josh'll probably stay up till the boys get through with their fire down there. He sort of has them on his mind," Lucy said. "Tell Harp I've forgotten all about the paint, and I didn't like the pattern very much anyway. I wish you wouldn't go; it's not late." Then she laughed. "Well, it is almost midnight, but you don't think of time a night like this."

"I know, it's a lovely night." Phyllis heard her own words. The evening hadn't been lovely. She felt uncomfortable in spite of Lucy's warm tone. On her way down to the house, she could see the fire in the meadow and thought of those boys telling each other what was wrong with them, their faces tight and closed to hide the hurt of some unpleasant truth, their eyes too eager, like Rich's. What could they tell each other? "I think you're a snob," perhaps, or "You're too ambitious." Could anyone tell someone he was cowardly? A boy would fight if he were called a coward, wouldn't he? Even at a truth-telling session.

But she was cowardly; she had always known it. Only James made her feel brave and proud. She hadn't been brave just now up there on the porch. Harp's spoiling Lucy's weaving had come to seem her fault, and then she had felt stiff and uncomfortable, the way she always did when she was in the wrong. She had felt as though Lucy resented their being here.

Now she was being foolish. Lucy wasn't like that. She was the finest woman Phyllis had ever known. Lucy never had to think of what she was doing or saying. She had a . . . a center; that was it, even aside from Josh. James, Phyllis thought, standing still in the middle of the path, was hers. She had none of her own.

She wished she had stayed up there on the porch with Lucy and Josh and James, even though she couldn't talk with them about other summer nights here.

When she thought back to a summer night on a porch, she remembered her mother sitting on the swing beside her, holding her hand and saying, "Your father isn't happy with me any more." Her mother couldn't say a hard, naked word like "unfaithful"; she couldn't say he was living with another woman, only "he isn't happy."

Phyllis distrusted that word still. It looked silly on a page with its two p's that gave it a fat-cheeked look and the dangling, coy y. After twenty odd years, thinking of her mother's words made her heart beat hard and the old tightness rise in her throat.

The sound of the big buses starting up from the corner was mixed in her mind with the silence that spread after her mother had said that. And the sound of the victrola playing in the apartment. She remembered guiltily that she had thought her mother might have put her mind to it and kept her father "happy," but she had known even at fourteen that her mother couldn't.

Why did she have to remember all that tonight? It was all over and done with, and her mother was dead. Her father was nothing at all like James, and she was very different from her mother. She had made sure of that. Harp had grown up without any worries about his parents . . . unless he wondered about James now.

Harp was asleep when she went in. He had his pillow over his head, a hot night like this. She lifted it away without waking him. Any other night, he would have jumped at the chance of sleeping on the porch at Ellie's, but tonight he couldn't face any of them. She knew how he felt. It would have been better if James had come down with him, but Ellie had come. Phyllis saw the two of them again, Harp stalking ahead, Ellie following. To halt her thoughts, Phyllis hunted for the book she had been reading.

Lucy went back to the porch, hardly listening to Josh and Jim, who were talking about the curious psychology of teen-age boys. She hoped Harp felt all right now. He had looked so miserable, and his mouth had worked as he told her about the accident. Of course, one had to be kind to children and understand why they did things.

She could remember when she was a child; the time she played with Aunt Mary's opera glasses, the ones that came in the dear little velvet bag, and had pearls on the handle. She had left them down by the brook and could never find them again, even though she had looked for days before she told anyone. She was so sure she had left them by a big white stone.

Aunt Mary hadn't believed her when she told her she had wanted to look at a minnow's eye, but it was true. Oh yes, she knew how Harp felt. And she had been fine and controlled about his spilling the paint . . . only, Harp had not quite believed her, and Phyllis had been uncomfortable. But Jim and Josh thought she was generous and kind. . . .

It was like old times to have Jim here. All those summers . . . Jim was hardly more than Rich's age when he first came. He was tall and thin and his suit was almost outgrown, she remembered, but he had seemed romantic to her because his father was a missionary off in India; someone her father had known in college. Dreadful to think that Jim's father had died out there in India.

"Would you like to be a missionary, Jim?" she had asked way back then, thinking, when she was sixteen, how exciting India must be and the conversion of the heathen from their idol worship.

"No," Jim had said, but he wouldn't talk about it.

And there had been the summer when she had wondered for a week or so if she were in love with Jim. Then Jim had gone back to summer school and she and her parents had gone to Europe. She had begun to get long letters from Josh, and Josh came over and met them in London. . . .

"It's cooler now," Josh said. "Too bad Phyl went down so early."

"I think she had Harp on her mind," Jim explained.

"You know it was partly my fault. I don't know why I didn't tell him to take the boat outside to paint it," Josh said.

Lucy pulled her chair forward as though the rockers were gouging the wall of the house. "Don't go on about it, please! It doesn't matter."

"Well," Jim said, "I hate to leave, but I think I'll say good night."

Lucy wondered if he was going because she had spoken so sharply. "Don't go," she said. She couldn't bear to have him leave yet; it had been such a bad evening.

"Let's walk over and see how the council fire is going, Jim," Josh suggested.

When they had gone, Lucy leaned her head back and closed her eyes, trying to rid herself of the sense of heaviness that seemed to fill the late summer night. There was no breeze, that was it. It would rain tomorrow.

"Looks as though they had decided to break up," Jim told her when he came back. "The fire is out and they're on their way up."

The boys were tired and disheveled as they came inside the circle of light from the post lamp. They looked sheepish and embarrassed.

"We put the fire out, Dad," Rich said. "The boys are gonna drive back."

"I thought you were going to sleep out around your fire," Josh said.

"Yeah, well we talked about it; I guess some of 'em gotta get back." Rich's careless speech sounded affected. What was the matter with him? Lucy wondered. "You guys all get in that one car?" he asked.

Boys were so dreadful looking at this age. The Lang boy was a sight with that soft beard and his hair too long.

Amazing that in two or three years they would be the object of someone's adoring love. Even Rich looked somehow unclean tonight. They all did, as though analyzing each other had left a kind of scum on them. A scum of egoism, that was it. Hearing your faults always made you more violently concerned with yourself. She was about to propound her theory to Jim and Josh, and then, instead, she went out to look at the weaving by herself.

As she turned the switch, she kept her eyes closed a minute. When she opened them, the paint splotch was still there. It had fallen on the finished weaving, rolled on the cloth beam, and must have run down through several thicknesses. She should have gone right at it with turpentine, but then Phyllis would have wanted to help, saying all the time how sorry she was. And she would have had to keep protesting that it was all right and that it didn't matter. Of course, it mattered. The whole summer's work was ruined.

Rubbing turpentine over the pattern ruffed the woolen threads, but some of the paint was coming out. She knelt on the bench and poured the turpentine straight from the bottle, not caring that it dribbled on the floor. The paint came out of some colors but was completely resistant in others. She could hardly see a trace of it on the dark blue.

She heard the boys' car and Jim and Josh calling good night to them. Rich's voice came after theirs, a little sulkily, she thought.

"Well, how was your party?" she heard Josh ask.

"It was O.K. I guess. I know one thing; I don't have many friends," Rich said.

"That's not the way to take it," Josh told him. "You have such good friends that you can talk frankly with each other."

"Not the way I see it," Rich answered. She heard his feet pounding up the outside stairs to his room.

"Rich, see here!" Josh went up after him.

Again the heaviness of the night came upon her. Now Rich was going into one of his moods, and that would bother Josh. And the paint was not coming out. The worst of the

78

stain was off, but the weaving was streaked. The blue looked dull and the light green was gray where she had rubbed so hard. There was no point in going on with it. But it was a pity to waste all that time and wool. Like losing the parts of the days she had spent here at the loom, parts of summer. She would cut it off right now and get rid of it, not have to come back out in the morning and find it still here.

In the box on the top shelf of the cupboard was a can of razor blades that she used for cutting threads. Then she noticed the machete Josh had brought back from the army, saying it would be so good for cutting brush, and never used, of course. She had to climb up on a stool to reach it. As she held it under the threads for a moment, she hesitated. The threads gave a soft final sound as they fell away from the blade. The edge wasn't as sharp, really, as a razor edge, and the handle was heavy, but it suited her.

"Are you out here, Lu?" Josh pushed open the door of the shed.

"Oh, Josh!" She dropped the machete on the uncut threads and covered her face.

"Lu, darling." Josh sat down on the bench beside her.

"I'm sorry to be so childish, Josh. It's just . . ."

"I know. I don't blame you. Anybody else would have blown up right there." He lifted her head from his shoulder to kiss her. "It was the cruelest piece of bad luck I ever heard of."

The minute Josh was there, knowing how she felt, she was all right again.

"I'm being perfectly ridiculous about it, but all of a sudden, Josh, I had to get it off the loom. And I didn't want Phyllis to see it again; it would make her feel so bad." But was that true? Had she really thought of that until now? She wished she wouldn't do that.

"Here, let me finish it for you" was all that Josh said. She sat and watched him cutting easily through the threads with the machete. His shadow moved behind him on the sloping roof of the shed, and the machete in his hand looked like some ancient halberd. Lucy laughed. "Josh, you should see yourself. You look like Bluebeard."

He made a lunge toward her, holding the machete high in his hand, and the shadow on the roof became an ogre. She cowered, holding her hands out before her, and her shadow was abject, cringing.

"Josh, do you know it's after one o'clock and here we are making shadow pictures. We're mad."

"Maybe. Who cares?" Josh hung the machete back on its hook. "Lucky thing I bought this instrument. I knew I'd need it for something." He screwed the cap on the turpentine bottle and put it back in the cupboard. The loom looked forlorn and empty with no weaving on it.

"I loved you, Lu, for handling Harp so gently. Poor kid, I almost wished Ellie had been the one to spill the paint."

"But, Josh, I was angry. When I came back out on the porch, I was trembling I was so furious. I told Phyllis I didn't mind but she could tell that I did, I'm afraid."

"You wouldn't be human if you didn't. She could certainly understand that."

"Yes, but . . ." Something had happened to the summer, to the four of them tonight, she felt.

Josh turned off the light. "Let's go to bed, Lucy Blair."

Twelve

JAMES WAS BENT OVER, polishing his shoes. "Do you see me as a research physicist in a laboratory? Josh paints such a picture he almost has me feeling this is what I was intended for from the beginning of time." His words had a slightly muffled tone.

"Yes, easily." Phyllis was standing in front of the greenish mirror trying to decide whether the Paisley dress was too dark for this summer night. His words brought her eyes quickly from the mirror.

"Old Joshua is far more confident than I am about this," he said as he stood up. "What all those laboratories want is young men just out of college or with an advanced degree. I made my decision a long time ago."

Phyllis looked hard at her own image in the wavy mirror. Because they were married that fall? If James had really wanted to go on, as Josh said he had always planned to do, he hadn't told her then.

"But," James said, "I suppose there's no harm in meeting Josh's friend."

"Of course not."

"It would be a relief to get away if . . ." He hung up the clothes he had taken off and transferred his cigarettes to the pocket of the coat he was wearing. When he put his hand into the other pocket, he brought out the agate. He looked up with a smile. "Did you put this in here?"

She opened the drawer to look for her earrings. "Lucy said you had left it the night Josh gave it to you and she thought you meant to take it."

"All right, I'll take it out and fondle it every other time I want to smoke tonight. You know, Josh believes there's

81

something you can *do* about everything. If you can't have a cigarette, you can rub an agate instead. It doesn't work that way. He's great, though, isn't he, Phyl?"

"Yes, he is, and he's so devoted to you."

"Amazing, too, after all I said about his book."

"Why, not a bit amazing . . ."

"Oh, well, Madam, I expect you to be prejudiced in my favor. It may be said that I count on it," James retorted with a flourish as he went out to talk to Ellie and Harp, who were eating there tonight.

"I'll be ready in a minute," she called, stepping into her bronze slippers, which were slightly scuffed, running a comb through her hair a last time, and leaning closer to the greenish mirror to bear down a little heavily with a bright lipstick.

"You look lovely, Aunt Phyllis," Ellie said as she came out. "I wish my hair was like yours."

Phyllis was touched by the unexpected compliment. "Thank you, Ellie, but I'll tell you a secret: I'd rather have long black braids."

"Uncle Jim says you're going to be highly dignified wogglebugs," Ellie said, giggling.

"And being wogglebugs is not my idea of a large evening!" James said with a face that produced more giggles. Then Phyllis saw that Harp was not laughing. His freckled face was watchful and his eyes followed James out the door.

"There's more chili, Harp, on the stove," she said quickly. "And more buns in the oven." Was Harp wondering how James could change so? Then Harp smiled his slow wide smile that was like James's.

She slipped her hand under James's arm as they went across the meadow, and felt his arm press her hand tightly against him. The lights from the house met them as they came toward the new stone steps that Josh and James had finished only that morning.

"Here we go, Mrs. Wogglebug." He stopped to light his cigarette, and she saw that his hand shook. Was it because he wanted this so much, or was it that he dreaded meeting people this summer? He wasn't really any better. But James said calmly enough, "I don't much like this social approach, but I would like to meet Ernest Hopkins. His lab's doing some interesting work in physical optics."

Lucy had said that morning, "I don't make anything of entertaining, really. And since Jim insists on supplying the wine . . . he really shouldn't do that, Phyllis."

"But he wanted to. He says it's to celebrate a friend's idiotic optimism."

"Not idiotic at all. Josh thinks this is a natural . . . and then you're making that fancy dessert so I'm only going to have to . . ." But she had disappeared into the pantry and the rest had been lost.

How sure Lucy's touch was, Phyllis thought when everyone went into the candlelighted dining room. The frosted grapes and the leaves from the woodbine that grew over the kitchen door, in a crystal bowl, insisted on an air of regality, and the fine old silver picked out the silver thread in the green cloth Lucy had woven in some more tranquil summer.

The Downeys were there, to give the casual touch, Lucy had said, and the Hopkinses. As they carried their plates outside, Mrs. Hopkins said to Phyllis, "You're from that good middle part of the country, I hear. These New Englanders think this is the *only* place, you know!" As she emphasized her words, her eyebrows rose and fell.

Mr. Hopkins carried Phyllis's wine for her and seated himself beside her at the long table set out on the flagstones. He was an unusual person, Josh had said, but she had not expected to feel it so clearly in his quiet voice and the intent look of his kindly sharp blue eyes and easy manner.

"You know," he told her, "Joshua and Lucy invite me over here because Josh feels the sciences need the gentler breath of the classics. But then, your husband is a physicist; does he manage to hold his own with the old Roman?"

"They argue with each other," she admitted, smiling. "But they're building a wall together. I think that's a good sign."

Hester Downey leaned over to say to Phyllis, "How much good the month has done your husband. He looked so tired when he first came, I thought."

"He had been working very hard before we left; the end of school is a bad time, but he's fine now," Phyllis said, glancing down the table to where James and Mrs. Hopkins were laughing at something Lucy had said. Fine now, fine now, sang deliriously in her brain. Oh yes, James must work with this man, with his intent blue gaze and high-domed forehead, and put all that went with Bellevue High behind him. Maybe that was the point of all of this terrible experience: to bring James here. But what about the boy? She wished she hadn't thought of the boy.

When he talked with James, Mr. Hopkins would see at once how bright he was. . . . Her proud swan feeling was descending on her, she thought with a secret smile. And the long glass table on the flagstones, with the pond lilies in the center, was rather like a lake. The light from the tall hurricane lamps reflected the lilies in the mirror beneath the glass, along with the darkness of the trees, so that the silver and glass seemed to rest on the surface of deep water. She sipped her wine and laughed at Sam Downey's story, but all the time she felt herself floating serenely through this pleasant world Josh and Lucy had brought about.

Ellie and Harpswell came to clear the table, bribed by promised rewards. Harp giggled with Ellie when Mr. Hopkins asked who these sprites were. "A fine young man you have there, Mrs. Cutler," he murmured to Phyllis, and she swam on down her proud course.

But it was the interested expression on James's face that gave the evening its clear sweet breath and touched the candle flames to sharper burning for her. She was startled to see him turning the agate in his fingers as he talked. What was it he had said earlier? "Josh believes there's something you can *do* about everything." Of course, and now James would see that Josh was right.

She was talking with Hester Downey when Mr. Hopkins's question caught her attention.

"You're a teacher, Mr. Cutler, can't you find a brilliant young student in your physics classes and send him down to us?"

James said, "The brilliant ones don't come along too often."

She could see him as he lighted his cigarette, his face illumined an instant, then seeming pale as the flame went out.

"That's just what James did do, Ernest," Josh said, and the sudden serious tone of his voice fell into silence.

Oh, he mustn't! Phyllis's mind cried out. James couldn't stand it. She put her hand under the edge of the table, which was all glass and iron again. But Josh was going on.

". . . worked with a boy who had unusual ability, tutored him so that he won the Enright four-year scholarship to Harvard."

"Splendid!" Mr. Hopkins murmured.

"I'm not through, Ernest," Josh said solemnly. "The boy didn't have the necessary moral fiber. He got mixed up with a girl and panicked at his first exam, and when he knew he had flunked it, he jumped off a bridge."

"How ghastly!" Hester Downey said faintly. Mrs. Hopkins clasped her hands in a sudden gesture. A sense of horror held them all for an instant as still as the flames inside the glass globes of the hurricane lamps. Darkness drifting down from the low-crouched hills walled them in.

The noise of Rich's car chugging up the drive clattered in on the silence. Rich came up the steps and stopped to speak to them all. His tennis racquets were under his arm, and the lights caught his fresh sunburn.

"Have a good set?" Sam Downey asked.

"Really good," Rich answered, then he said with a grin, "Jim, I'm afraid I didn't get that physics problem worked out, though," and ducked inside the house.

"All right, Rich, you've warned me," James called after him, and everyone laughed.

"What a hard experience for your husband, Mrs. Cutler," Mr. Hopkins said under cover of the laughter.

"Yes," Phyllis said.

"Yes, we've been swimming in the Quarry hole. I loved it," she said in answer to Sam Downey's question. She saw James's face with that closed look, and when Lucy went to get the coffee, she followed her. "Let me, Lucy. I . . ." she began.

"I know," Lucy said. "But it's all right, Phyl. Josh thinks Jim must get so he can talk about it, then he won't brood over it so."

When she came back out, Mr. Hopkins and James were talking together down by the new steps. James was all right, wasn't he? Josh had known what he was doing? Then she saw that James had gone off and left his agate again on the table. She picked it up and put it in her pocket.

Thirteen

THE TROUBLE with having come here almost every summer of her life, Lucy thought, was the way a new day could seem like some other day, years ago, and then she had to puzzle about it underneath this day's happenings. Sometimes, she knew in a flash: this was like the day they went for a picnic to Loden's Pond years ago, or the day Tony, the horse, was sold; but other times, like today, there was just the teasing sense of some other time.

Lucy measured the coffee and set four places at the table. With breakfast this early, Josh and Jim were going to get started before the day really warmed up. They ought to be able to get into New York State before it was hot. Jim's appointment with the lab was for three o'clock.

Someone, Rich, probably, had left an empty pop bottle on the sink board, and a little trail of crumbs. He must have come down after everyone was in bed and had pop and a doughnut, or perhaps he was up early this morning. At that age, a stomach could stand anything, but when there was a pitcher of milk right in the refrigerator, why didn't he have sense enough to drink milk instead?

And eggs and bacon. Josh would want a hearty breakfast. She laid the sliced bacon in the cold iron skillet. That other day it must have been early, too, with the sun not reaching the high dresser against the wall, or the old rocker, so the kitchen was still cool and shadowy.

Had she been here alone? One of those times when she had come down before anyone was awake and tiptoed through the house feeling it a little sad without anyone in it. She wondered if Ellie ever had that feeling. Maybe Rich did. She picked up the sticky pop bottle to put it in the case in the shed and then went out on the flagstones to look across to the mountain. Like this it must have been; so fresh and lovely they should all be up every morning at this time. She should be, anyway, like her father. She could remember how he used to seem to be returning from another world when he came back from an early-morning tramp. Josh did that, too, but differently, and Josh liked to have the whole family up.

What was it about that day? Something not quite good, something sad. The bacon was starting to cook. She turned to go in when she saw Rich, way down along the bank of the brook. She saw him running, and then he was out of sight. Rich was rather like her father; he went off by himself the same way. Josh minded his spending so much time on that old car, but he did these other things, too.

As she came back into the kitchen and met the mingled coffee and bacon smell, she had a queasy feeling in her stomach, as though she were pregnant again. She turned the bacon, not quite looking at it, and poured herself a cup of coffee. She glanced at the clock. It was twenty of six; maybe she better see that Josh was up. Then that whole other morning came back, the summer she was fourteen.

Her father was taking her to Miss Ingalls's School for Girls. They had had an early breakfast, and she remembered coming down to the kitchen and being nauseated by the smell of bacon, and looking at the clock to see how soon they would have to leave. She had gone outside, just as she had this morning, and thought that the next time she looked out across the meadow she would have been there and come back and nothing would ever be the same. "Of course you want to go to Miss Ingalls'," her mother had said. "Don't be foolish, dear. All your new clothes are ready."

"Uniforms," she had answered, hating her mother that moment, and when she glanced at her father, he was eating his breakfast as though he didn't care about her at all. Now the whole anguish of that day came rushing back into her mind. As she took the bacon out, she remembered standing stiffly beside Miss Ingalls, looking out through the door at other girls passing in the hall. She had no desire to know any of them.

"She may have trouble in algebra," Miss Ingalls had said, "but I am sure she is going to work hard." Of course she would have trouble. She could never understand the algebra originals, and someone would explain them to her and she still wouldn't understand and have to say that she did for fear the person would think she was stupid.

Then Miss Ingalls had said, "You will want to walk out to the car with your father." But as they went along the corridor, she kept measuring the distance to the end of the hall where the sun burst in through the screen door and made a coppery square on the polished floor. She caught hold of the rough stuff of her father's coat sleeve, and her father felt her touch and took her arm, but she couldn't look up at him. When they were outside, she would tell him she wouldn't stay here; she would work on algebra every day at the farm if she could only go back with him. The gravel was hard to walk on in her hateful new brown ox- fords, and she kicked it just a little with her toe so the sharp pebble left a scar on the new leather. Father saw her do it and didn't say not to. Then they came to their car with the license plate that had the only friendly combina- tion of figures in the world.

"Well, Lucy," her father had said. "We're going to miss you around home." She had never heard her father's voice sound like that. She could not think of anything to say. "Mother will be glad that your roommate's mother went to Miss Ingalls'," and it was as though they both knew that the kind of thing that mattered to Mother didn't matter to them.

She managed to look quickly at her father's face. His eyes had a funny, damp look about them. He hated to go away and leave her. He was going to miss her. There wouldn't be anybody to ride with him at the farm or to play checkers. It was going to be really lonesome for him at home. And he was getting old. She wondered now how old her father must have been then . . . not more than forty-five. But she remembered feeling that she must do something to make it easier for him, so he wouldn't look so sorrowful. It would be better if he left now, but still he didn't start the car. Then she saw her bathing cap on the ledge above the back seat.

"My bathing cap!" she said, pointing to it and laughing as though it were a joke. "You might have gone all the way home with it." And when she came out with it, she said, "Wasn't it lucky I saw it," though, of course, she didn't really care about any old bathing cap.

Then her father started the car, and she stepped back and smiled for all she was worth and waved the bathing cap as the car started to move.

"Good! The coffee's ready," Josh said as he came into the kitchen.

The four of them joked about the trip at breakfast. Only once were they serious.

"After Jim looks into this physical optics stuff, he'll come back with a new vision," Josh said, enjoying his pun.

"I suppose that's what I came to you for in the first place," James said, and for a long moment the four of them were held together in the warm circle of yellow light from the old-fashioned extension lamp above the table. The morning sun coming in across the sink was thin and pale beside that light, and only reached part way over the blue board floor, leaving uncertain shadows by the tall dresser. Lucy caught Phyllis's eyes and smiled.

"You know, I won't have the faintest idea what these birds are talking about when they get into that fancy infrared stuff," Josh said.

James finished his coffee and took out a cigarette.

"No you don't! We're on our way right now." Josh pushed back his chair. "Don't expect us before we get here, Lucy. We may get lost in New York."

"Come on up when you get ready, and we'll go swimming," Lucy said to Phyllis as they stood there after Josh and James drove off. "We'll have a lovely, lazy day."

Phyllis wished she could have gone with them. Just when James had said, "Bye, Swannie," and kissed her, a sudden unexpected panic had caught her. She snatched a piece of the lemon verbena bush, no blossoms, but dark-red seed pods now, and ran to the car to give it to him. "Here, James, for luck. You can still smell it."

"All right, for luck," he said, putting it in his pocket.

"It's good for them to go off like that. They'll have a chance to talk," Lucy said. "Getting them off seemed like the year Josh taught in summer school and only came up weekends."

"Didn't you hate it?"

"No, it was strenuous, but he enjoyed it," Lucy said.

As she went down to get breakfast for Harp, Phyllis wondered why she couldn't be as casual as Lucy about things. She was utterly ridiculous; James would be back tomorrow. He and Josh would have such a good time, as Lucy said.

The mist was lifting from the top of the mountain; the sun caught the far trees in light and left the low fields still dark. Green, green everywhere, all shades and textures, from the light pulpy green leaves to polished dark ones. Sometimes she felt there was too much of it here, rising in waves around her; color of life . . . wasn't that what poets called it? . . . color of jealousy . . . which was it? Hiding the sky and the plain black-brown earth and the rocks, not as clothes covered your body, but as talk and silences hid your feeling. Even in this minute, the sun seized on the rags of cobweb spread over the wet grass and showed the green beneath.

The small living room was empty. There was the rain-coat James had decided not to take with him. As she hung it away in the closet, she remembered how James had asked, "You'd like this, Phyl, if there should be an opening, wouldn't you?" And she had answered so quickly, "Oh yes, James. I could leave Bellevue without any regrets, couldn't you?"

He had been looking in the mirror then. "I don't know that I'd say quite that. I'd like this work if it's what I think it is." Then he had said, "It might seem like running out on something to give up the job there just because of Leonard."

"Why, no it wouldn't. That has nothing to do with it," she had said, a little frightened that James should say the boy's name just now. But then she had seen the clock face, and she had said, "It's six-thirty, James. Lucy will have breakfast ready."

Why had she hurried him? They should have talked it out then. She wanted to say she didn't care what he did so long as he wasn't depressed. Why hadn't she told him that? All that mattered in the world was being with him. But that was the way she had done that other time.

Harp was awake, and she could talk with him while he had his breakfast, and after that there were the beds to make and the tiger lilies to throw out, which had looked so proud when she cut them yesterday. Today, they had shrunk into tight curled wads of themselves. But in spite of all the things she did, she kept remembering.

Her mother had gone to Union Station with her and stood there, so she had turned quickly from the window the minute the train began to move. She couldn't bear to see her standing there alone. Her mother had talked all the time they were waiting about how exciting it was to go on the sleeper, and only at the end had she said, "If they ask, tell them I'm fine and very busy. Tell your father I like working for Dr. Knowles. Other peoples' troubles take your mind off your own." But, of course, she wouldn't tell him that, and it wasn't really true, because everyone's troubles only seemed to connect with the fact of her father's leaving. It was always there in the tone of her mother's voice when she said things like "When I see what other people go through" or "He calls up all the time to ask about his wife, poor man." Mother was always saying of her position as Dr. Knowles's receptionist, "Of course, it might seem dull to your father's wife, but I feel I've been very, very fortunate."

It had been exciting to go off alone when she was fourteen. She remembered how the man next to her had told her the train was all aluminum and it was hundreds of pounds lighter than the old trains. She had shivered to think of the shell of the train no thicker than the aluminum saucepan above the stove, but that was better than thinking how it would be to get off and meet her father, and his wife, whom she had never seen. She had hoped, *hoped* he would come alone to meet her.

Just remembering that time made her so nervous she had to go to the lavatory, as she had had to before the train pulled in. When she washed her hands, they were as cold as they had been then, too. She put eggs on to boil for the picnic lunch she and Lucy and the children were going to have and stood stupidly, watching them, but her thoughts went right back to that other time.

Her father had been alone at the train to meet her. She had seen him far down at the other end and looked away, pretending that she hadn't seen him, and then let her eyes find him again. Then she had started to run and flung her arms around him and clung to him there in the station. "Father, it's been so lonesome without you," she had whispered against his ear. "I want to stay with you all the time." He had held her so tightly that she had not realized until later that he hadn't answered that, hadn't said she could. He gave her his handkerchief that was so decently different from a woman's. They had walked away together with her hand on her father's arm, and their steps just matched.

"Laura is going to meet us for luncheon at one-thirty," he said. "She's delighted that you came." They didn't say any more as they walked across the parking lot and found the car.

"It's a new car, Father!" She was disappointed that it wasn't still the green one she remembered, that she had always thought of as theirs.

"I hope your mother bought a car," he said.

"No. Mother doesn't want to have to take care of it alone."

"I'm sorry about that; it would be good for her. She was

always timid about taking any responsibility. How is she?"

"She's fine," she said.

"How is school?" he asked after a little.

"It's fine." She thought of Jane Ford asking her in Latin class if her mother and father were divorced, and later she had seen her whispering to Pat Allen.

When they parked across from the insurance building where her father had his new office, he sat there a moment before he got out.

"Phyllis, you know I'm sorry it has to be this way. I miss you, too, terribly, but . . ."

She held her hands between her knees because she was afraid the trembliness inside would show outside, and stared at the clock on the dashboard.

"We're late. It's quarter of two," she said. Her father would have gone on sitting there talking to her; he would have forgotten all about Laura, but when she said that, he got right out.

Why did she do that? Why did she always bring time into something that was more important than time?

"Laura, this is Phyllis" was all her father said when they met in the restaurant. Laura did not offer to kiss her, just shook hands and smiled.

"Hello, Phyllis. I've wanted to meet you for a long time," she said.

She wasn't as pretty as Mother, and she even looked older, but she was more interesting to talk to, Phyllis thought, and then was angry at having thought it. Laura talked to her as if she were grown up. "You are old enough to understand some things that your mother is unable to see," she told her.

They went to the art museum and the symphony concert and out to dinner. Phyllis often found her father's eyes on her, and he played Russian bank with her, as he used to. They went to a movie by themselves because Laura said she had seen it and it was too good for them to miss. Phyllis stayed two weeks.

Her father was to pick her up at the apartment to take her to the train, but he called just before the time and explained that a client had flown in and he couldn't leave, so he had to say good-by on the phone. "Lots of love, Phyllis. Come soon again. Tell your mother I'm very proud of her daughter and that she's doing a fine job. Will you remember to tell her that?"

"I guess so," she mumbled because she could hardly speak.

Laura looked up from her desk when she was through. "I'm afraid he thinks it would be too hard to say good-by to you." She didn't want Laura to see her cry so she didn't try to say anything. "Don't cling so hard to your father, Phyllis; you can love him more when you don't."

Laura went down to the street with her and put her in a taxi. "Good-by, Phyllis," she said, shaking her hand. "It's good to see how adequate you are. Come any time. We'll always be glad to see you."

Phyllis took the eggs off the stove and poured cold water on them and began to chip off the thin shell with her fingernails.

Having James away made everything she did seem pointless, merely a kind of marking time, except for thinking how she would tell him about it when he came. Already she had begun shaping the narrative of the day in her mind for him. "After you and Josh drove away . . ." she would say, "I came down here and felt so surrounded by all that green I got so depressed. Don't laugh, James, there *is* too much of it; it's everywhere . . ."

Once, when they lay together in the richly idle ease of having loved, she had said to James, "No one looking at me could tell I was so foolish, really, could he? I mean, I look adequate enough?" James had hid her face in his shoulder and smoothed her hair as though she were still that child she had been and said, "You are adequate; completely and beautifully so." His using the word gave it back its natural virtue again.

"And then," she would tell him in her recital of the day's happenings, "I heard Harp calling . . ."

When she went out, Rich was there holding a raccoon with a belt fastened over his sharp snout. Ferocious fear looked out of the animal's bright eyes but his paws seemed to clutch at Rich's jacket sleeve like the hands of a child, except that the fingers were almost as long as a woman's. The bush of a tail hung down under Rich's arm. The raccoon was tensely still one moment and the next made a desperate jerk, but Rich had him tied into his jacket.

"Rich, wherever did you find him?"

Ellie couldn't wait to tell the saga. "Way up on the brook, Aunt Phyllis. He was gone so long Harp and I went to find him and he had the raccoon."

"Look, Mom," Harp pointed out, "he has my belt around his nose."

They made a procession up to the house for Lucy to see, and told the story of the chase and capture all over again, with embellishments.

"Look at that tail go. See, Aunt Lucy, he's angry!" Harp pointed out.

"Where do you think I better put him?" Rich asked.

"Put him in that box you had your pigeons in for now. If you keep him, you'll have to fix a cage," Lucy said.

"Keep him! Of course we are, aren't we, Rich?" Ellie cried.

"We could keep him down at our house if you can't," Harp offered.

Rich's hand tightened on the strap around the raccoon's nose, and he looked up at Lucy with a pleased smile. "Won't Dad and Jim be surprised!"

"We all went swimming," she would tell James. "And after the children went back up, Lucy and I stretched out on that big rock by the pool."

All around them the green stillness of the woods held cool shadows, and the depths of the water were cold. Only on the rock and the merest surface of the pool the sun burned hot. For a long time they lay without talking.

"I'm beginning to feel like part of this rock," Lucy said. "As though I could lie here through heat and cold and rain, even snow. Did you ever feel that way?"

"No," Phyllis said. "Not rock . . . wind, maybe. Sometimes I can lose myself in it—along Lake Michigan when there's a real gale—not even feel the ground. But nothing so secure and permanent as rock. I don't need that old tombstone verse up in the cemetery to tell me that where they are now, there I will be."

Lucy sat up on the rock and unpinned her hair, letting it fall down her back, and, as though pulled by the weight of it, she dropped her head so the sun struck full on her closed eyelids and high cheekbones and throat. Then she opened her eyes. "That doesn't worry me; this is so good right now, it's almost enough."

"Oh, it's never enough!" Phyllis could hear her own voice. It was too vehement. She spoke more quietly when she said, "This is lovely, but all the time I've been lying here, I keep wondering about James; how the day is going for him."

"Of course," Lucy said, as though that was only natural. "But you don't need to be anxious, Phyl. Ernest wouldn't have phoned to ask Jim to go down and see him if he hadn't meant to offer him a place. And Josh will see that he comes out all right."

"I know. I'm being foolish . . . but when James left this morning, I felt I could hardly stand it." She laughed. How had she happened to say that? What was Lucy thinking? Phyllis slid down off the rock and stood leaning against it, watching the smooth brown surface of the swimming hole give back a dim reflection of the sky.

"I wonder if all children of divorced parents sound as I do or whether I'm neurotic." She made her tone brittle and amused and skipped it across the stillness.

"Don't worry, you're not. And Jim adores you." Lucy's tone was warm and light. They were both skipping sentences now, on the surface.

"James always says you're so exactly right for Josh," Phyllis offered in return.

*

It turned cold that evening, cold enough to have a fire, and Phyllis lingered after Harp and Ellie had gone off to bed and Rich had gone up to study. The day had been long and lazy, yet strung taut, Phyllis felt, between the absence of the men on their particular errand and the capture of the raccoon.

Now, sitting here by the fire, they talked of the children and small domesticities, but what they had said by the pool still lay in their minds. Lucy was knitting, Phyllis was mending socks.

"You know, if Jim takes a job with Perkins-Elmer Labs, you can both come up here every summer," Lucy said.

"James has always wanted that brick house about a mile from here," Phyllis said. "Maybe we could buy it some time."

Tomorrow she would tell James, "We had such a good time talking. I really felt I came to know Lucy."

They heard a sudden scratching sound.

"That's the raccoon trying to get out," Lucy said. "Rich shouldn't have left the box there on the porch."

Fourteen

L U C Y   L I K E D the steady sound of the rain: thumping on the long porch roof, slapping against the flagstones, and drumming so loudly on the canvas awning it drowned out the restless clawing of the raccoon at the wire of his cage. It was raining so hard she couldn't see beyond the stone wall to the south, and the bottle-green maples were the farthest boundary to the east.

These all-day rains were a part of summer. She had no sympathy with the children if they grumbled. If they took books from the old bookcases and curled up in odd corners to read, she had a deep sense of pleasure, as though she were reading the books herself. She liked having everyone home, scattered over the place, as they were now. Josh was working away in his study, and she sat at the desk between the two front windows of the living room, feeling as though she were at the pilot's post watching the boat plow through the wet green seas of grass. Magwitch lay curled on one corner of the desk and added to her sense of contentment.

She heard the study door open and Ellie say, "He won't eat, Dad. I've tried everything. I gave him the dog food and the lettuce and some salmon."

"Did he eat anything this morning?" Josh asked.

"Harp said he ate a piece of chicken, but I don't believe him."

Josh ignored the last remark. "Well, I'll have a look at him."

They went past Lucy's windows as though they were walking the deck of her ship, Ellie talking busily and Josh giving all his attention. Josh and the boys had built a cage for the raccoon just under the side steps.

They were there so long Lucy went over to the south window to see if they were out in the rain. Of course Josh was standing right out in it. She stepped out on the deck and now she could hear the poor animal racing up and down.

"Come look at him, Lucy. You won't get wet, you can stand under the awning. He looks thin, doesn't he?"

"Yes," she admitted. "His fur looks sick."

"And he won't play with anything hardly," Ellie mourned.

"Don't give him any more things like my glass paperweight to try him out," Lucy warned.

"I gave him Jim's lighter yesterday," Josh said.

"Josh, you sinner, what did Jim say?"

"Said the raccoon needed the cigarettes to go with it."

Then Rich appeared, coming up from the guesthouse, where he had been working physics problems with Jim. He was scowling. "Why don't you let the poor devil alone? It maddens him to have people fussing over him. A raccoon isn't like a rabbit or a chicken or something. He's a wild animal," Rich grumbled.

Josh looked at his son. "All right, Ellie, I guess we'll let Rich take care of the raccoon after this."

"Well, I just mean . . . you can't organize a wild animal like you can children."

Josh went into the house. Ellie trailed off toward Phyllis's house. Lucy waited a moment, watching Rich stoop down by the cage. "Hello, you masked man, you," he murmured to the raccoon.

Josh had closed the study door behind him, she noticed. Rich was rude, but she was glad Josh hadn't said any more to him. Of course, Josh was as excited about the animal as any of the children and had made a special trip to the village library to see if they had any books on raccoons. She supposed that was what put Rich off, and having to build a cage for him according to specifications. Rich had no business being so selfish. After all, if they were going to have the animal, Ellie and Harp . . . and Josh could have

100

some fun out of it. It would be better to get rid of him than to have so much trouble.

She heard the big desk chair, which had been her father's, squeak as Josh tipped back in it. It squeaked restlessly again and then the study door opened. Josh came out chewing at the heavy plastic bows of his reading glasses.

"Young boor, isn't he?" he asked as he had asked her judgment on the raccoon.

"He was ashamed of himself right after he said that. I suppose he caught it and he thinks it's his in some special way. I was glad you didn't say anything more." But she could see that wasn't what was bothering Josh, so she said, "Come and have some tea if you're taking a break."

He followed her out to the kitchen and sat down at the table while she put water on to boil. His hands played steadily with his glasses. Finally he said, "Do you want to know a nice irony? According to my plan, I'm supposed to be writing the chapter on decisions; you know, some of the famous ones in classical history and then go on to talk about how a young man must make up his mind and commit himself to his decision. And here I sit watching a man who can't make a decision. It makes me sick to see Jim, Lucy."

Lucy poured the water into the teapot. "It's strange, too, because we thought he was so interested when you came back, so pleased to have them make him such a fair offer."

"It's the kind of work he always wanted to do. From the way he's worked up over this boy, you can see that teaching isn't the right thing for him. He'd make as much as he does in that high school; in time, he'd make more. I don't see what makes him hesitate."

"But he hasn't absolutely decided against it, Josh."

"No. He just looks troubled and keeps saying, 'I don't know. I just don't know.' He seems worse off than before he had this chance. The morning after he got back here, something seemed to hit him and he's been in a funk ever since."

"It isn't Phyllis's fault," Lucy said. "She was so happy about the whole thing."

101

"She goes around looking down in the mouth, too," Josh grumbled.

Lucy changed the subject. "How long before he has to let them know?"

"Fortunately, Ernest told him to take his time to think it over, but I'm sure he expected to hear from him by now. It's been over a week since we were there. The good thing is that Ernest really wants him. He told me Jim showed an unusual grasp when he was talking to him."

Lucy filled their cups, and they sat drinking their tea in silence, but she could hear the raccoon springing at the wire of his cage.

"If the raccoon doesn't get used to that cage pretty soon, you'll have to move it farther away from the house," Lucy said.

Josh's cup scraped against the pottery saucer. "Lu, weren't you talking about going to a weaving exhibit over in Manchester?"

"Oh yes, but I'm not going."

"I wish you would, and take Phyllis along with you. Stay overnight and make a real expedition out of it. I'd like a chance to be here with Jim, just the two of us, the way we used to be when we'd come up here from college."

Lucy shook her head. "Phyl won't want to do that, Josh. She isn't the least bit interested in weaving and she was terribly tense when Jim was away last time."

"I'll tell her why I want her to go. Maybe Jim feels her anxiety. I'm sure I would. It would be good for him to be here without her. Anyway, it's worth a try. I tell you I'm worried about him, Lucy. He seems so wrapped up in his own thoughts I can hardly get to him."

Lucy said quickly, "No. Let me tell Phyllis. Josh, you can only do so much, you know. You can't make Jim completely over."

"I don't want to make him over; I just want to help him back where he used to be."

Fifteen

PHYLLIS PICKED UP her bag and came out into the living room where James sat leafing through the pages of a magazine. "All ready?" he asked.

"Oh, James, I don't want to go on this trip. I don't care any more about a weaving exhibit than the man in the moon."

"Lucy wants you to go; you can't very well disappoint her. And you'll see some beautiful country down there."

Who cared about the scenery? She couldn't keep from asking, "Will you be all right?"

"Of course, Phyl, don't be silly."

The very naturalness of the remark sent her spirits up in an instant and spurred her on to say, "Write the letter while I'm gone, James. I do think it would be exciting to go there."

James bent down to put the magazine under the table. "No. I'm not going to write until Sunday; that will be the fifteenth. Anyway, Hopkins told me to take my time. I don't believe I'm going to take the job."

His face had changed; sobered somehow. His tone was flat. He looked so troubled she wanted to tell him it didn't matter to her, but she looked away from him out into the orchard and was silent.

"I'm sorry to be so trying, Phyl, but I've got to do what seems right," James added.

But there wasn't any right or wrong about it. Now he had worried and twisted things around in his mind so that it was a moral issue. He was thinking about the boy again. Couldn't he ever forget about him? She tried to keep her hopeless feeling out of her voice. "It isn't a question of right or wrong, James, at all. It's simply a matter of what you want to do." She sat down in the chair across from him. She couldn't go off on any trip and leave him like this. James was just sitting there with his face half hidden by his hand. "James! Don't you see?"

James took his hand away from his face. "Well, don't worry about it, Phyl. I just didn't want you to get your hopes set on my going with the lab."

She heard Harp and Ellie calling outside the house, and said, "You and Josh can talk about it." But her hopeless feeling was in her voice.

Harp's voice sounded far away. "Mom!"

"Hurry up, Aunt Phyllis," Ellie called, and James went to the door to answer them. They walked back up with the children.

Josh must have sensed their mood, Phyllis thought, because he began making great sounds of jollity. "You two *Hausfraus* look pretty fetching!" he said. "Just dropping the cares of domesticity off your shoulders and deserting us. Phyl, I'm trusting you not to let Lucy come back with a new loom strapped on top of the car."

Phyllis found it an effort to answer in the same vein. "I may not be able to control her. Don't you and James get into trouble."

They were in the car when Ellie remembered she had forgotten something and had to run back. Phyllis looked over at James standing there in his plaid shirt and old khakis. He was watching the raccoon in Rich's arms. Rich could take it out now, holding the leash that fastened to the leather collar.

Josh said, "Don't you think we ought to have a picture of the girls as they go off?"

"Here, Jim, hold Raccy while I go get my camera," Rich said, giving the animal to James.

Phyllis and Lucy posed, holding their handkerchiefs far out the window of the station wagon and grinning. Phyllis's last glimpse as they drove off was of James holding the raccoon. The bright animal eyes were anxious above the comical mask. James was smiling but his smile seemed like a

104

mask, too, slipped over the sober look she had seen on his face at the cottage.

"You know those boys can't wait for us to get off," Lucy said. "They're going straight back to their college days and have the best old time. They came up one spring vacation and batched it and . . ." Why would they want to go back to their college days? Phyllis wondered.

Lucy dropped Harp and Ellie off at the Downeys', where they were going to stay overnight, and then she and Phyllis were free to talk of anything, but conversation trickled slowly. Then Lucy said, "Look at that first flash of scarlet over on the hill. Wait till you see the color this fall."

Phyllis was slow in answering. "I don't believe we'll be here to see it. James said this morning that he didn't think he'd take the position. I think we'll be going home, as we planned, the end of August." She listened to herself say the words.

"But didn't you think he was steamed up about it when he and Josh first got back?"

"Yes, I did," Phyllis admitted. "But the next morning, he seemed awfully depressed. He hasn't talked about it all week, and I didn't want to make it harder for him by asking."

"Of course not. But I know Josh feels that this is a real opportunity and he's going to be terribly disappointed if James doesn't take it."

They drove the length of a village street before Phyllis managed to say, "I know Josh must be out of patience after he got Mr. Hopkins interested and drove James down there. . . ."

"Don't worry about that," Lucy interrupted. "He's only thinking of what's best for Jim. But why is it, Phyl? Why would he turn it down?"

"I think he feels . . ." Phyllis hesitated, but it was a relief to talk to Lucy. "Oh, I think it's all because of that boy. You know what he said that night we heard him telling Josh about it. He feels so responsible for his death. . . ."

Lucy dropped her hands from the wheel an instant. "I

know but isn't that absolutely absurd? I mean, after all, anybody who knew James `Cutler would know he would never force a boy against his will!"

"It's so terrible to see him, Lucy," Phyllis cried out. "James feels he was so intent on having the boy do him credit that he wasn't thinking of him as a human being." It was hard to explain James to Lucy because it was difficult for her to understand how he felt. There was that time at home, just after the boy's death, when James took off his shirt and said, "You're surprised when you take your clothes off to find them stained and sweaty; that's the way I am to find out that what I thought was my noble interest in Leonard could be plain, self-seeking pride. But I couldn't see it until it was too late."

"He's mad," Lucy said out of the silence. "On this one thing, I mean, for I've always thought he was about the sanest person I've ever known, next to Josh."

Phyllis watched the road turning, turning, never running straight for long, always shut off by a hill or caught in the shade of close-growing trees, until they drove down the wide main street of Manchester.

"You listen to the lecture, Lucy," Phyllis said when they had parked the car. "I'll just amuse myself at the exhibit."

Women have such a passion for a pattern in their lives, she thought, lingering to watch the woman in Puritan garb weaving at an eighteenth-century loom. So many threads . . .

"Made of linen, the warp is, made from their own flax," the weaver was explaining, "and the woof is wool." A woman standing beside Phyllis made a gesture with her hands so that the Mexican silver bracelets on her arms clashed together. "They must have worked from sunup till sundown!"

"And then by rush light or whale oil," someone added.

The bracelets clashed again. "I suppose it was their life, you know."

A woman tamped out her cigarette and threw it in the

106

old dye kettle on the ground. "Well, it would give her a chance to rest, just sitting there pushing that shuttle through."

Someone laughed derisively. "Wouldn't be so bad if she watched television at the same time."

"But, seriously, you know I think a woman's happier doing things with her hands, don't you?" The person who asked the question thrust her own hand in the pocket of her well-tailored shorts for her cigarettes and lifted her bronzed leg to scratch her match on the sole of her sandal. "I think a woman's just made that way, just as she's intended to bear children."

Someone in the group turned to her with a smile. "Ought to keep her from wringing her hands, anyway," and the small group laughed as they moved on past Phyllis.

Did she wring her hands? Phyllis thought, and looked down at her left hand ringed with James's wedding ring. Ring-wring, her mind teased.

She could still hear the woman in shorts impressing her point on the group. "But there really is something restorative about work with your hands. You can feel it in your soul."

"Where do you suppose they got the names for their spreads?" a woman asked Phyllis. "I don't make up my patterns, but if I did, I'd never be able to give them such romantic names. There doesn't seem to be any connection with the design."

"Maybe there is a connection with what they thought as they wove," Phyllis suggested, wondering what name Lucy would give to the design she wove this summer.

"Where's the Bird of Paradise in that?" Phyllis's companion asked. "Double Chariot Wheels, about 1830; that must have been woven down South where they were used to those spirituals, not up around Vermont," Phyllis's companion remarked. Out of what prosaic life did that woman lift herself to think of Chariot Wheels, Phyllis wondered. "Isle of Patmos" . . . somebody who read John's Revelations tried to catch them in a web of thread.

"Now the Lovers' Knot, I can see that, some young girl, likely," the woman said. It seemed to Phyllis suddenly that the minds of women long dead came too warmly alive as she stood fingering the soft, rich web of their dreaming. "Natchez Trace and Lee's Surrender" . . . more than the memory caught in the colored threads.

But what happened if you couldn't make a design? Or if somebody spilled paint on your pattern and you had to cut it all off? When she had gone out to the shed the very next day, the loom had stood bare. She hadn't wanted to ask Lucy about it. Harp had seen the loom, too, and asked her privately if he had spoiled the whole thing. She had tried to comfort him because he had been uncomfortable with Lucy ever since. "It wasn't just your fault, Harp," Phyllis had heard herself saying. "Why wasn't it?" Harp had asked. "We should have been sure where you were painting," she had told him lamely, but that hadn't been the reason. Sometime she would say something to Lucy about it; maybe on the way home.

"The colors they used then are better than the new dyes, with all they know about chemistry," someone said. "Look how bright after all these years." A table displayed the common weeds from which the old dyes came: spiderwort and tansy, black-eyed Susan and ordinary alder bark. Phyllis found herself mouthing the names, letting them run over her tongue like some ancient charm against witches, or ague . . . or fear.

"They used everything, didn't they?" her companion interrupted. "Didn't have to import things. Anything they wanted they just went out and found it."

Then Phyllis had had enough. She had no desire to hear the decorative woman in the tweed dress she had woven herself tell how to make your own designs. Instead, she walked down the village street, past the splendor of the famous hotel with its Negro porters out in front rushing to open the doors of the cars that stopped. Difficult to help people wriggling out of the little foreign cars or the long low models, she thought. More point to such courtesies when

108

the guests had come in the hotel surrey to stay for a week or a month and lifted long skirts over the carriage step. She walked past the shops full of things she had no desire to buy, trying to fasten her attention on an old doorway, or the seventeenth-century date in a brick wall. A telephone caged in steel and glass mocked her from the front of the drugstore. If she could just call James and hear his voice! But Josh and James were hiking up the mountain now. She had to get through dinner and the night before she and Lucy could leave.

"Josh likes motels, where you can get out so easily in the morning and don't have to bother with bellhops and trail through a hotel lobby, but I must confess I like a little elegance now and then," Lucy said as she climbed into the high tester bed. "The town is so crowded we were lucky to get this room even with the double bed."

Phyllis turned out the light and got in on the other side. The maple leaves beyond the window waved in shadow on the wallpaper and the balled fringes of the canopy moved ever so slightly in the half-dark room.

Lucy said, "The boys have a good night to sleep out on the mountain. Only I don't suppose they'll do too much sleeping."

Phyllis remembered the night Rich and his friends held their truth party by the campfire in the meadow. Would it be like that? "It should be heavenly up there," she said.

After a long pause, Lucy said, "It's so good for them to be off by themselves. Josh is awfully glad to have this chance. He's been waiting for the right time to really talk because he feels he must make James realize how necessary it is for him to get away from that school."

"If he can just convince him," Phyllis said.

"Josh is used to helping people see a way out of their problems, you know."

Phyllis said, "But James isn't . . ."

"People, of course. I didn't mean that! But Jim above everyone. Josh told me one time about how Jim wasn't going to join a fraternity . . . didn't believe in them and all that sort of thing, and Josh made him see why he should."

"But that was different. That was when they were boys," Phyllis objected.

"Yes, I know, but Josh can make him see this, too."

Phyllis felt the faint irritation in Lucy's voice. How tiresome they must seem to her. And James's wavering back and forth . . . like the shadowy movement on the wall. The words sprang out without her meaning to say them: "I feel you and Josh are giving up your whole summer to us and our problems." She writhed at the apologetic tone of her own voice.

Lucy's voice was warm. "Phyl, how can I make you understand that Josh and I love you both. The idea of giving up anything doesn't enter into the picture at all." She leaned over and kissed Phyllis. "Don't be foolish." Then she turned over, arranging her pillow noisily.

Phyllis turned on her side, moving a little closer to the outside. Lucy's words were comforting, but the sudden kiss embarrassed her. She couldn't find anything to say, and she was unsure of her own voice. She needn't be uncomfortable, or apologetic. "Josh and I love you both . . ." Lucy had said. It was so amazing.

The silence grew softly in the room. She wished the room were dark, not half dark like this. She felt strange sleeping with Lucy . . . as though the awareness in their bodies of lying, Lucy with Josh, she with James, made them secretive or shy. No . . . that wasn't what separated them and made their talk dwindle into uneasy silence. It was—wasn't it?—that they were not quite comfortable with each other because their minds held secret the things Josh and James had said? Lucy was hiding Josh's impatience; she had felt it even though Lucy denied it. And she herself was keeping deep buried the wild things James said. Their minds were secret and turned away.

If she and Lucy were girls again, they might have told each other the things they thought, even twined their arms around each other; she wished she had had Lucy for her own friend . . . but she was the wife of James's friend. They weren't girls, and what they thought was touched by an awareness of what James and Josh thought.

Lucy made her voice sound sleepy. "This is just like sleeping at a house party."

Phyllis made an assenting sound in her throat. She had not gone to house parties as a girl. She had lived at home when she went to college, and slept in the same room with her mother, in the bed that used to be her father's.

Long after they had said good night, Phyllis felt their wakefulness in the dark, the way you could feel a moth in the dark, soft and still, but live, on a window curtain.

Josh came down to the car when they got back. "Welcome home. You made good time."

"We were afraid you would still be up on the mountain and forget that you had wives," Lucy said. She could see that Josh was disturbed. His tone was a little too hearty. When he lost sleep, he showed it more than he used to; maybe that was all it was.

"I didn't let her buy a loom, Josh," Phyllis managed to say before she asked, "Where's James?"

"He decided to go over the other side and come down that way."

Lucy's surprise lined her voice, "Why, Josh, that's five miles more around, at least."

Josh's voice had a dry edge. "Well, Jim likes to hike; he said he wanted to go that way again. I'd had enough, so I came home on the old trail."

"Why, you softie," Lucy said quickly, trying to make it a joke. That wasn't like Josh. Hadn't they got on together? "Let's have tea, and maybe Jim will be back in time. When did you leave there?"

But Josh had gone around to take out their bags. Phyllis caught hold of his arm. "Josh, was James all right?" Her eyes were wide in their anxiety.

"Of course." Lucy felt his irritation and hoped that

111

Phyllis didn't. "You should have seen him finish up the pan-cakes, and they were good ones, Mama, even if you do think I make 'em too thick."

He realized he had sounded short and was making up for it. Lucy let her voice sound a little ecstatic, "Was it wonderful up there last night?"

"Nice, all right," Josh said briefly. "We saw a couple of deer, one of 'em standing drinking in that spring."

"What luck!" she said. "Jim must have been delighted." Then what was the trouble? Phyllis was starting down to her house. "Come on back up and have tea; don't stop to change, Phyl." She turned to Josh. "We didn't stop anywhere because it looked like rain." Had Phyllis answered? She hadn't heard her. "We didn't stop for Harp and Ellie because the Downeys said they'd bring them home. Is Rich back?" She wouldn't ask Josh anything about Jim yet. She went out to put the kettle on. Josh followed her to the kitchen and walked over to the window. He was just standing there, looking out at the mountain.

"You never saw such beautiful weaving," she went on. "Maybe next summer if nothing happens I'll go over there and take some lessons." The phrase "if nothing happens" hung in her mind. What had happened this summer? "I think Phyllis enjoyed the trip, too. We had a lovely room. . . ."

Josh took a glass from the cupboard. "I'd rather have a drink, Lucy. I imagine Jim would, too, if he gets here."

"All right. Maybe Phyllis would. But Jim will be lucky if he makes it in time for dinner."

Josh said, "He'll come when he gets here." He finished fixing his drink. "I'm reading over some stuff; if you don't mind, Lu, I think I'll take this in the study. I can't take Phyllis's looking like some kind of a frightened animal when she thinks something's wrong with Jim. Her worry is half his trouble."

"She's so wrapped up in him, she can't help it," Lucy said.

Phyllis hadn't come, so she went on upstairs and changed her suit. Of a sudden, she was tired. It seemed like an ordeal

112

to get dinner and try to pull the evening together. Perhaps she should say something to Phyllis about not asking Josh about Jim now, not till after dinner anyway. But why was he so upset?

She heard the Downeys drive into the yard with the children, and called to them from the window.

"We can't stay," Sam called back. "We're just getting out to see this raccoon we've been hearing about."

She was on her way downstairs when she heard Ellie cry out. Harp came running into the house. "Uncle Josh, Aunt Lucy, Raccy's gone! The door of the cage is wide open."

They stood around the cage, examining the door catch. "Someone must have closed the door but forgotten to fasten the chain afterward," Sam announced.

"But who would do that? Who put him in last?" Harp wanted to know.

"I think your father was holding him as you drove off," Josh said. "And then we left right after that. No one was here to take him out again."

"He must have thought he had fastened the chain and not quite caught it; that's so easy to do," Lucy said. Harp looked as though he was going to cry. She was startled when she glanced at Ellie. Ellie's eyes had that secret look they could get.

"That's a shame," Sam said. "The children said it was so bright."

"Yes, he was," Josh said. "I've never seen Rich so fond of anything."

Lucy saw Ellie walking off toward the steps that led to the orchard. She said quickly, "Ellie, come here, dear."

Sixteen

PHYLLIS MADE HER FEET walk slowly down the path, but in reality she was running headlong, as she had run in her childhood down the block their apartment house was on. She dropped her bag by the door and went in to sit on her bed in the room that was the innermost recess of the house.

Something was wrong with James. Why hadn't Josh gone with him; why would he let him go alone? Was it because James had told him he wasn't going to take Mr. Hopkins's offer, and Josh was angry? No, not angry . . . disappointed.

She must go to meet him. The trail must come down out of that green wilderness to the highway somewhere. If James wasn't on the highway, she would start up the trail. She was getting into a shirt and jeans, hurrying so fast she put the shirt on wrong side out, when she heard the children calling. Harp could go with her.

"I'm gonna ask her," she heard Harp say. Harp and Ellie were scuffling and Ellie was trying to hold her hand over Harp's mouth when she looked out. "Harp, you said you wouldn't!" Ellie screamed at him.

"Harp, stop that," Phyllis said. "What's the matter?"

The children stood apart. Ellie's eyes filled with tears and she fingered one braid. Harp's face was red.

Harp said, "Well, I'm going to."

"Going to what?" Phyllis demanded.

"Mom," Harp began, but Ellie interrupted. "You said you wouldn't if I told you!"

"Ellie, suppose you tell me what has happened." Some

114

new fear joined the fear about James; Phyllis felt herself trembling.

Ellie curled her bare toes into the rug and glanced quickly at her and then away. "Mother said I couldn't."

Harp said, "Ellie heard Dad say it was a shame to keep Raccy caged up, and she thinks he let him loose. Dad wouldn't do that, would he, Mom?" He seemed almost to plead with her.

Phyllis found Lucy and Josh in the study. "Josh, what happened? I'm terribly worried about James. I can't believe he would let Rich's raccoon loose." She knew she was talking too fast, but she had to speak fast.

"Oh, Phyl, the raccoon got out by himself, I presume." Lucy sounded as though she were trying to calm one of the children. "He was always working at the fastening. Anyway . . ."

"Phyllis, sit down a minute," Josh said.

She sat down on the chair by the door and faced him, and then because his face was so stern she looked past him at the pieces of a cream pitcher that lay on the table waiting to be mended.

"I had a long talk with James last night up on the mountain. . . ." Josh was so deliberate she clasped her hands together and held them between her knees to keep them still. "He said things to me and I said things to him. I won't go into that. If I believed as he does, I would have to give up trying to advise any boy again. I'd have to throw away this whole manuscript." His hand rested a minute on the thick pile of pages on his desk. "And I may, as it is. But I don't happen to feel the way he does. I think James is not himself."

"But . . ." she started to break in, but Josh seemed not to hear her. He was looking out the window as though he saw James as he used to be.

"Jim was always an extremely sensitive person, and he's brooded over that boy's death. He's almost pathologic."

The word "pathologic" terrified her. "You see why I'm so worried about him, Josh."

115

He faced her so quickly. "That's exactly it, Phyllis." His hand came down flat on the pile of his manuscript, knocking the pages out of line. She watched him even them, making each edge meet the edge of the next. What was? What did he mean? He was looking down at the pages now. "I think you've made his condition worse by worrying so over him."

Had she really heard him? He meant . . . She rubbed her hand down over her cheek to hold her mouth steady because she felt it trembling.

"You know?"—Josh sounded as though he hardly knew her, as though she were a pupil—"you can exacerbate a situation by fear. In fact, you can bring a condition about by fear alone. You've been so afraid he was going over the edge, you've brought him to the brink of it."

She caught her breath. Lucy's chair creaked as though she were going to stop Josh, but he went on.

"I'm not saying, Phyllis, that you did it consciously, but subconsciously. You were so afraid people in that school or the parents of that boy would think that James was responsible that you made James feel that he was."

She looked over at Lucy, waiting for her to deny what Josh was saying. "I know," Lucy had said the other day when she told her she was worrying about James. Lucy must know that she didn't bother James with her worry. But Lucy was silent. Her eyes were looking out the window. Phyllis tried to bring her own eyes back to Josh, but, instead, they found the clock on the desk. It was ten after six; it must have been five after six when Josh said that.

Harp's voice came clearly into the room. "He did not!"

Lucy went out, and Phyllis felt deserted.

Josh turned around in his chair. "Jim told me something about the pressures of that job of his, Phyllis; I'm not sure that your interest in having Jim succeed there didn't serve as part of the pressure. . . ."

"James never said that!" Someone else seemed to cry out with her voice.

"No, of course not. He isn't aware of his whole situation there, but I can see a great deal that he doesn't."

116

His voice was calm and cold. His face seemed larger as she stared at it; his eyes seemed hardly to see her. How had he used to look sitting across the room from James when they were in college? "You know how I feel about Josh," James had said. She tried to remember how Josh had looked that night, the night of Ellie's birthday party, when she told him how worried she was, and he had put his arm around her and said he didn't wonder, that he would want her to come to him. In a minute, Josh's face would gentle and his eyes would warm and look right at her.

"This letting the raccoon go is obvious to me," he went on. "Jim is so locked up in himself, he never stopped to think how much it meant to the kids, or that it was Rich's property. He thought of the animal's being forced to stay in a cage and he's so obsessed with his fantasy about forcing that boy that he leaves the cage unfastened so the raccoon can go free."

She watched Josh pick up his glasses and fold and refold the bows.

"He's quite right, you know, Phyllis; there are all kinds of cages. You can make one by your fears about him."

He meant . . . that she had made a cage. He didn't know anything about it. "It's such a freedom, loving you," James had said once. But that was before all this. Had she made a cage? She stared back at Josh, but she couldn't see his whole face. Her eyes moved from his eyes to his high brow then down to his hands. She felt him waiting for her to say something.

She stood up. "Thank you," she said, not knowing why she was saying it. "For telling me these things." She heard Lucy in the kitchen. Lucy didn't believe what Josh had said. Last night, Lucy had said, "How can I make you understand that Josh and I love you both?" Phyllis hesitated in the doorway of the study, wanting to go to Lucy, waiting for Lucy to come to her. Then Lucy came out with a bowl in her hands. "Phyllis, take some fresh raspberries down for your supper" was all she said.

"No thank you. I have everything I need," she called back. When she went down the porch steps, she had to go around and look at the raccoon's cage. The double wire door stood open. She stooped down so she could see his den in the farthest corner of his run, where it was almost dark and he could hide from people.

Rich drove by the house with a flourish and waved when he saw her. "Hi, Phyllis!"

What did Rich think about James's letting the raccoon go? She couldn't face him now. Again she felt she was running, although she walked down the stone steps James had helped Josh build. Would Rich ever forgive James? James must have been . . . out of his mind to do a thing like that. Her face moved queerly so she could feel her mouth drawing down. She buttoned the top button of her shirt and turned the collar up because her throat ached. She mustn't let Harp worry about James. Her mother had always shared her worries about her father: "Your father didn't use to be like this," her mother had repeated so many times it had become a refrain.

All the time she was getting supper for Harp, she kept her mind away from Josh, from what he had said. But everything she did had a sense of strangeness about it: pouring milk into a glass, slicing bread, standing in the doorway and calling out into the rain for Harp. When had the rain begun? She touched her hair and found it wet. So it must have been raining when she came back from . . .

Harp could only talk about the raccoon.

"I imagine Dad thought the chain was caught and it wasn't. He'll feel dreadful when he finds Raccy gone," she said, looking across the table at Harp. His face was sober and accusing.

"Ellie says he was sort of patting him like he hated to have him shut up."

"Dad loves animals."

"But Ellie says in a special sort of way," he insisted, "as though maybe he was planning to let him go."

"Well, when he gets home, you can ask him," she said. "Do you want to go with me to see if we can meet Dad and save him that walk along the highway?"

"Sure. Do you know where he'll come out?"

"No, but we can try."

When they came to the village, she let Harp run in to the store to ask, though she wanted to herself. "There isn't much of a trail down that side, Mom. A man that was in there said a person could come out most anywhere once he was down far enough."

"Well," she heard herself saying, "we'll try it anyway. She turned on the radio so she wouldn't have to talk and drove slowly, watching every break in the woods that might mean a path. Back home, the sky came down cleanly to the land, and you could see as long as there was any light left, but here, the close-growing green made a snare to hide the light. Already, it was dark where the branches interlaced. The clock on the dashboard showed five of eight.

"He better come pretty soon or he'll get lost in the woods," Harp said.

"Oh, he won't get lost. If it gets too dark, he'll just lie down and sleep in his sleeping bag."

"Are you worried, Mom?"

"No, of course not. Why?"

"Your voice sounds kind of funny."

She switched the radio station. There was no point in going any farther. "We might as well turn around, don't you think, Harp?" She didn't look up into the woods now. They were too dark. She kept her eyes on the highway, almost thinking she saw James once. "You can bring a condition about by fear alone," Josh had said. "You've been so afraid, you've brought him to the brink. . . ."

"Mom, you're driving pretty fast. You got up to sixty and we're almost to the village limits."

"Am I? Well, I'll slow down. I was trying to keep up with the windshield wiper, I guess."

She drove slowly through the village. "You'll know this village before the summer's out," James had said the day they arrived.

"Harp, isn't there a road that comes in closer to our end of the pasture, so we don't have to go way up around the drive?"

"Yes, but it's all grown up and you have to open the gate."

"You can open the gate. I've always wanted to drive in this way," she said. After Harp was asleep, if James hadn't come, she would go out again.

Harp went to sleep too soon, and then she was alone. The rain made a steady hissing sound on the orchard grass. Surely, James would have found a shelter and holed in for the night. He was good out in the woods. Of course he was all right, but he must know she would worry. . . . "I think you've made his condition worse by worrying . . ."

She had never hurt James with her fears. She had kept them to herself, except when she told them to Josh and Lucy. The minute James got back, they would leave here. Josh didn't know anything about her life with James. She grabbed up her raincoat and went out again.

She drove five miles along the highway and then stopped the car. The wiper banged noisily back and forth. James wouldn't come out above that point, surely, but instead of turning around, she stepped on the accelerator and kept going.

"There are all kinds of cages . . . you can make one by your fears about him . . . your interest in having James succeed . . . part of the pressure. I can see a great deal that he doesn't. I'm not saying that you did it consciously, but subconsciously. You made James feel . . . responsible." The phrases kept coming with the strokes of the windshield wiper. She beat her fists against the wheel until they hurt and the car slewed so she had to steady it.

"James!" she cried aloud in the car. "James, where are you?"

Two cars passed her, and she watched for James in their headlights, but the road was empty, with the white line dividing it into two wet black slides.

The road brought her into a town, and the signpost caught by the headlights told her she had gone eighteen miles. She turned around and started back.

Why had she ever called Josh and told him about James?

That had been wrong in the first place; letting James think that Josh just happened to call him. Because she had been frightened about James's depression, that was why she had called. He hadn't helped James. "Josh thinks there's something you can do about everything," James had said. She tried to remember the exact tone of his voice when he said that. He had meant that there wasn't anything Josh could do this time. Nothing she could do either.

Had James felt caged? Was that why he had let the raccoon go? She thought of him standing there holding the animal as they drove off. "This letting the raccoon go is obvious to me," Josh had said.

She came again to their village, and drove down the main street, looking at the houses that were already dark, and at the house where the light came through the fan window in the hall. Oh yes, she knew the town very well now. When James and Josh and Lucy used to come here in winter with their skis, laughing and joking and stopping in the store to buy provisions, they never thought a thing like this could happen. If James had never met her and never taken the job in Bellevue, this never would have happened. That was what Josh thought; and that was why Lucy was silent. She left the village behind and drove out the road to the farm.

Lucy was waiting for her when she came in. Her tone was matter-of-fact. "Phyl, I came down to tell you Rich and Josh started out right after dinner to find Jim. Of course they're crazy to go in the rain, because Jim is perfectly all right and delighted to have another night up there, but Josh wouldn't listen to me."

Phyllis took off her raincoat without answering.

"It will be an awfully hard trip at night, about ten miles before they're through. . . ."

Phyllis spread her coat over the back of a chair. "Thank you for coming down to tell me," she said without looking at Lucy.

"Phyl, please remember this, it's because Josh cares so much about Jim that he said those things. He's terribly upset. Then when you burst in this afternoon and said you were so worried . . . well, you can see how it made him feel."

Phyllis stood by the table, straightening the lamp shade. Why couldn't Josh and Lucy realize that whatever she did was because she was terribly upset, too? "I'll try to remember not to bother him with my worries again," she said.

Lucy stood up to go. "Try to sleep, Phyl. They'll all camp up there overnight, so don't stay up."

Perhaps she should have stayed with Phyllis, Lucy thought as she went back through the rain to the house. Phyllis must have been just driving along the highway, hoping to see Jim. But Phyllis was in no mood to talk. Of course, she was terribly keyed up . . . and angry because Josh had talked to her so . . . frankly. The house felt damp and chilly. She made a fire in the study and drew the curtains against the dark rain. She could ask Phyllis up here, but she doubted if Phyllis would come tonight. Anyway, she felt too jangled to have her. How could Jim do such a thoughtless thing? "I can't stay here and let him go wandering around alone up there," Josh had said.

The sound of a step startled her, and she spoke quickly. "Is that you, Ellie?"

Ellie appeared in the door, in her pajamas. "I thought I heard a fire down here." She sat cross-legged in the old leather-tufted chair the children always called the "elephant."

"Ellie, you can't wait up for them," Lucy said.

"I just want to stay a little bit. Mother, do you know what I was thinking?"

"No." She could do without Ellie's thoughts tonight.

"I was thinking what if Uncle Jim got lost up there and a wild animal, a wildcat or a lynx or something, should spring on him and he'd have to fight him bare-handed. . . ." Ellie was sitting up very straight, her eyes seeing it all before her.

"Wildcats and lynx are the same thing, Ellie."

"But I mean what if Raccy, who's gone back to the

woods, appeared and recognized Uncle Jim as the one who let him free and . . ."

"Ellie, suppose we just stop talking about the raccoon altogether. And I don't want you to say a word about it to Harp or Phyllis or Jim."

Ellie stared into the fire. "I'm not going to."

"Go on now, Ellie, please." She let a little impatience barb her words.

Ellie came to kiss her in a sudden burst of affection. When she reached the stairs, she called back again, "Mother, do you think Uncle Jim is all right?"

"I imagine he's in his sleeping bag by now under some big pine tree just as snug as a bug. And Dad and Rich are hunting him everywhere," she added.

Once, she went out on the porch to see if Phyllis's lights were still on. She could tell by the bright patch they always made on the rough bark of the apple tree. Phyllis would be just sitting there, worrying, going over every word Josh had said. She might run down and say, "Phyllis, come up and wait with me." But she hesitated.

Phyllis had no idea how upset Josh was that Jim had as good as decided to go back to that school. "Some masochistic idea of torturing himself," Josh had said angrily. You had to know Josh to understand how he was when he cared so about a person and couldn't do anything to help him.

She went back in to the study. That was what Jim had said when her father died and Josh was so broken up he seemed angry. "You have to know Josh, Lu. He was so sure they could save your father."

"But," she had protested, "the doctor said there wasn't much hope. We knew the operation was only a chance." She had sat here in this room late that night talking to Jim.

"Josh heard him, Lucy, but he didn't really believe him, don't you see?" Jim had explained. "There's something unconquerable about Josh; he always thinks there's a way. That's what I love about him." Jim's saying that had helped her. That was the way Josh was, and she loved it in him, too, but it made it hard for him.

She picked up her raincoat to go down and talk to Phyllis. "Jim understands Josh," she would say. "When Josh gets impatient with Jim over his smoking, Jim doesn't get hurt."

But when she stood out on the porch, the light patch had disappeared from the apple tree. Phyllis must have gone on to bed.

She turned back into the house and closed the door. It had swelled with the rain, as usual, so she had to slam it. The sound carried above the rain. She took off her coat slowly. If Jim understood him, what had happened up on the mountain so that they had separated? Josh hadn't told her.

Lucy left a light burning in the kitchen even though they couldn't get back tonight, then she went on up to bed.

Seventeen

JAMES ARRIVED HOME before the other two. He came walking across the field like a man who has been tramping a long time, setting one foot down after the other, doggedly, not caring what they stepped on. His pack seemed molded into his back. His hat was dark with the rain and made a shadow across his face now in the morning light. His head was bent a little as though to balance the weight on his shoulders.

Phyllis saw him before he reached the orchard, and went running to him through the wet grass.

"James!" she called, her heart leaping within her so the word was half a cry.

"Hi," James said. "Watch out, I'm soaked. You'll get wet."

"Oh James, are you all right?" She forgot to try to keep the fear out of her voice, clinging to his wet arm as they went up to the house.

"Kinda bushed, otherwise I'm all right. If the rain hadn't come down so hard, I'd have been back last night, but I couldn't see a thing. I've got to go up and tell Josh. He'll be fit to be tied."

She had forgotten Josh. "He went out to find you, James, he and Rich. They left right after dinner last night."

"Why the crazy fool, he might have known he couldn't find me in the dark. I didn't stick to the directions he gave me, anyway. I decided to cut south and make my own way down. But it was all overgrown and tangled in there. Lots of new growth since I've been on that side of the mountain."

He sat down in the kitchen and dropped his sodden hat

on the floor. He was soaked through to the skin, and water dripped from his pack. As he unlaced his boots, water ran through the lacings. "I'll have a cup of coffee if you have some, then I'll go tell Lu I'm back."

"You get your things off. I'll go up," Phyllis said.

"Where's Harp?"

"Off exploring some place with Ellie." This was not the time to tell him she had heard them plotting to find another raccoon. "Did you sleep at all last night?"

James grinned. "Oh, I got under some big pine trees against a rock, but it wasn't exactly dry. No, I didn't sleep much, as a matter of fact."

There was something different about him, she thought as she started his breakfast. Some quietness, or was it just his tiredness? His damp hair looked black against his skin, and he seemed to have lost the tan he had. He seemed still to be up there on the mountain, or still thinking about it.

"You shouldn't have separated," she said. "You could have got lost."

"I think I'd have found my way out eventually. Josh wanted to come right back down. I wanted to come down the other way by myself. I don't suppose I'll get up there for another fifteen years."

What did he mean? she wondered as she went up to tell Lucy. What had they said to each other, he and Josh? Had Josh said if it weren't for your wife, you wouldn't have made so much over this? No, he wouldn't say that to James . . . but what if he had? What would James say? Would he say Phyl only worries when I do . . . Phyl and I are so close. . . .

Phyllis heard the wooden bump of the loom before she reached the top of the steps. The lattice was thrown open, and Lucy sat there with the sun on her back. How could she go right on with what she was doing? Didn't Lucy know that they had come to the end of . . . of any possible understanding or affection or even decency? What if James had told her she was driving Josh crazy? Would she go on being calm and tranquil?

Phyllis moved a little closer, stepping softly on the grass,

so she could see Lucy's face from the side. She had begun
to feel she knew Lucy; she had even told her how she felt
about James. And Lucy had said, "I know," but she didn't.
She was sorry she had told Lucy anything. Probably Lucy
had told Josh what she said. Phyllis watched her hands moving so surely, her strong face, which never sprang into a
telltale flush when she was excited, but kept its cool, tanned
composure. Why hadn't James married Lucy? He would
have lived here where he could go up the mountain whenever he wanted to, and never been hagridden by an anxious
wife.

Lucy turned quickly. "Oh, Phyl, you startled me. I don't
hear anyone coming with the loom going."

"You're at it early," Phyllis said. "The weaving exhibit
must have inspired you."

Lucy shrugged. "Keeps me busy while I'm waiting for
those crazy men." Her smile was warm.

"James is back. He just got here."

Lucy took her hands off the loom. "Is he all right?"

"Tired and wet, but he's all right. He was—" she hesitated over "angry" and said "sorry"—"sorry that Josh
and Rich had gone after him because he said there wasn't
much chance of their finding him in the dark. He cut down
to the south where there wasn't any trail."

Lucy's tone changed. "Didn't he realize that Josh would
be rather worried about him?"

Phyllis spoke before she thought. "Josh should know it
isn't good for James to feel people's worry." She looked
away from Lucy as she said it, then she managed a thin
laugh that was hidden under the wooden bump of the loom
as Lucy began weaving again. She felt awkward standing
there. "They'll be along soon now," she said, making her
voice blithe.

"Oh yes, they'll be along." Lucy's tone was even more
blithe and cool.

Phyllis waited, drawn in spite of herself toward Lucy,
her anger and hurt almost lost in some feeling of liking,
even of admiration, that had grown with the summer. Then
her anger flooded back into her mind as she remembered

how Lucy had sat still in the study and let Josh say those things.

"Well, don't *you* worry about them!" Phyllis said, loud enough so that her words carried over the sound of the loom. She walked quickly away. Why was Lucy weaving a brand-new pattern? Surely, all the weaving on the loom hadn't been ruined.

As she passed the porch, Phyllis felt the emptiness of the raccoon's cage without looking in it. Still, it was better not to hear the scrabbling sounds of his claws on the wire. And what could they have done with him at the end of the summer? Maybe James hadn't meant to let him out at all. Maybe Raccy was just clever enough to get out of his cage by himself. "There are all kinds of cages," Josh had said. Certainly there were. Everything could be a cage, for that matter: the guesthouse, "where you can be as independent as calves in clover," was tight and terrifying to her now, and this orchard, which had seemed so heavenly free that first morning, was one. The grass was barred by the shadows of the trees and roofed over by the thick pattern of the leaves.

The apples on that one tree looked red enough to eat, but they weren't. The fruit was hard and sour. She picked an apple and bit into it, setting her teeth on edge and swallowing the piece before she threw the apple in the grass. She would *ask* James if he felt he was in a cage. What had happened to make her hesitate to ask him things? No two people in the world were so free as she and James.

"James!" she called when she came to the door of the little house.

But he was asleep, lying across the bed, spread-eagled, as Harp lay often, the pillow bunched under his head. She touched his head, which was still damp. His face was tanned; why had she thought it was pale this morning? But it had a worn look, and the creases cut down too deeply to the mouth. He didn't look as though he knew her, any more than a photograph of a person did. He looked alone by himself. He must be too hot with the blanket pulled up over his shoulder, but she left it. She pulled the shade to darken the

128

room and picked up his wet clothes, which lay in a heap. They smelled of sweet fern and swamp mud or brook and the tangled brush he had come through rather than of any taint of his own body, she thought as she carried them out to the shed.

She and Harp were having lunch when James came out.

"Gee, Dad," Harp said, "you sure scared everybody. Mom and I drove up and down all night to see if you'd come out on the highway, and Uncle Josh and Rich went after you and everything."

James smiled. "I'll tell you a secret, Harp. I almost scared myself. I did get lost up there. I went without a compass and I got down in some timber that was so thick I couldn't see where I was going. It's a wonder I didn't come out over in New Hampshire. But I saw six deer and I slept in a spot under some pines where deer had lain."

"Did you see any raccoons?" Phyllis saw Harp's eyes sharpen with his thought. She poured the coffee, watching the steaming liquid mount inside the cup.

"No, Harp, I didn't."

"You know Raccy's gone. He got out," Harp said.

"Did he? Well, he was a smart one."

Phyllis felt Harp looking at her and avoided his glance, waiting for him to ask James outright if he let him out. But he didn't.

"Do you know whether Josh and Rich are back?" James asked.

"Yup. They were here when Ellie an' I got home," Harp said.

"Wasn't that just like that old Saint Bernard to start back up the mountain in the dark to find me?" He said it as though it were something wonderful. "Rich is going to be another one just like him—" he qualified it—"in a way. Josh thinks I'm crazy and he can't understand what I'm driving at some of the time, but he'd drag himself up a mountain in the rain without a moment's hesitation. Wasn't that fine of him, Harp?"

Maybe he was just saying that for Harp, Phyllis thought.

When Harp ran off to ride the jeep into town, they still sat at the table. In a minute now she would tell James what Josh had said. She began to shape the words in her mind: "I know Josh is just as generous as he can be but . . ." No, he hadn't been generous about her. He hadn't stopped to think how she felt. "Josh thinks the world of you, James, but he resents me. He thinks I've imprisoned you in a cage of my fears. . . ." She couldn't breathe freely until James had answered her. He wouldn't stop to answer. He would press his lips hard on hers and say, "What do you think?" the way he had stopped other silly questions.

James's face was grave, suddenly. "I'm afraid I hurt Josh."

"Good," she wanted to say. "He hurt me." She had never kept anything that worried her from him in all the years she had known James.

"He thinks I've changed, and he's right. Good God, after this experience with Leonard, I can't look at things in the same way. You know, Phyl, it was a queer thing; we started out arguing about my taking the job with the laboratory and we ended up talking about ourselves. He said some things I couldn't go along with. . . ."

Had Josh told James what he thought about her? James wouldn't let him say those things. . . .

". . . and I said some things I wish I hadn't."

"You mean you quarreled?" A hideous eagerness sprang up in her mind.

"No. Josh and I couldn't ever quarrel, really. But we sat there making statements. I never thought we could get to the place where neither of us could see why the other felt the way he did about something."

"James, let's go now. Right away. I feel we've been here a long time. . . ." Too long, she was about to say.

"No, Phyl. I don't want to leave before we planned. That's only a couple of weeks. I don't want to go away from here with Josh feeling the way he does. It would be a different kind of world if anything really happened between us."

She got up and went outside, but James went on sitting there as though he didn't know she had left.

130

Eighteen

"'IS JIM BACK?'" Josh asked before he even opened the screen door to the kitchen. He looked terrible, Lucy thought. She saw Ellie staring at him and didn't want her to see him looking that way, as a mother must want to keep her child from seeing its father drunk. Rich looked tired, too, and soaked, and burned red from the sun the day before, but Josh's skin seemed drawn too tight over his face, his eyes avoided hers, and his voice was dry, as though it hurt to talk.

"Jim got here about three hours ago," Lucy told him. "Did you and Rich have a bad time?"

He let Rich answer. "Did we ever," Rich said. "We must have gone ten miles over that old mountain. But it was fun. I liked it."

Josh peeled off his torn shirt. "I take it he was all right."

"Jim? Oh yes, he was fine, I guess," Lucy said. "Phyllis came up to tell me he was here, and Harp said he went to bed and slept as soon as he had something to eat. I should think you two would be ready for bed." She took pains to sound as though this were any camping trip.

"I'm not tired," Josh said. "We slept last night after we knew we couldn't find Jim. We could stand some food, though."

Josh seemed abstracted even when Ellie threw her arms around his neck. "Did you see any wild animals, Dad?" she wanted to know.

"Several deer and a porcupine," Josh told her, not bothering to make them sound exciting for her the way he usually did.

"We saw a big black bear, Ellie, and it was coming right toward us in the dark!" Rich teased.

"You didn't either! Did you ask Uncle Jim, Dad?"

"Ask him what?"

"About Raccy? Did he let him out?"

"Ellie, what did I say about . . ." Lucy began, but Josh interrupted. "He didn't admit to leaving the cage open intentionally. He said he supposed he could have. Let Ellie ask him if she wants to."

Lucy spoke quickly. "Oh no, Josh. I don't want her to do that. Just let's drop the whole thing."

Rich clapped his hand to his mouth in mock horror. "Do you know what? I was supposed to take Barbara Corey to the barn dance last night!"

"Yes," Ellie told him. "And Harp and I saw her at the post office and she asked where you were."

"Excuse me!" Rich rushed out the door.

"Mother, can we have them up and cook steaks outside tonight? Can we?" Ellie demanded.

Lucy hesitated. Yesterday, she had told Ellie they could all have dinner together when they got back, but now . . .

"Uncle Jim and Aunt Phyllis haven't been up here to eat for ages, and you said," Ellie persisted.

"Oh, Ellie, I don't know about tonight. Everyone needs to rest up after that trip." Josh certainly did, though she wouldn't say that, of course. He hated ever to admit being tired. But tonight it was more than tiredness. He was just standing there, studying the calendar on the wall by the sink. Whatever had happened on the mountain, Josh wasn't going to feel any better about it until he did see Jim. She had said she would ask them. She turned to Ellie. "Maybe you're right, Ellie. Maybe this is the night to celebrate their return. You go and ask Aunt Phyllis and Uncle Jim, and tell them that."

"They may not want to come," Josh said from the doorway.

"Of course they will. What an idea!" But Lucy heard again the sharp tone of Phyllis's voice when she had told her James was back, and remembered the way Phyllis had come up so quietly and stood watching her. "Hurry down as soon as you change and we'll have something to eat," she called after Josh. But as she laid mats on the table and set their places, she went on thinking about Phyllis.

She should have talked frankly to Phyllis right then; she should have said, "Phyl, I know that what Josh said hurt you, but you want him to tell you how you can help Jim most. . . ." She heard the reasonable tone of her own voice as she could have said it. "Josh thinks . . ." But Phyllis knew exactly what Josh thought, and she was angry about it. There was no point in saying it again.

Was Josh right about Phyl? The question held her mind fixed, helpless as one of Ellie's dragonflies, impaled on a pin, only her mind wasn't lifeless; her thoughts still moved their wings laboriously. Josh blamed Phyl for making Jim feel guilty because of her worry over what people thought. But would Phyl care about anyone but Jim, really? Things Phyl had told her, impressions of Phyl and Jim together reflected themselves on the gossamer surface of Lucy's thoughts.

The screen door banged behind Ellie. "They're coming," she announced. Lucy was relieved, and when Josh sat down at the table, she said, "They're delighted to come."

"Dad," Ellie asked, "have you ever gone over to the other side of the mountain, where Uncle Jim came down?"

"I've taken the trail, Ellie," Josh said. "I can't say that I've ever been lost and wandered all over that wilderness area. That's not my idea of a true Mountain Man."

Ellie giggled. "Uncle Jim's all scratched up. He said he got into blackberry bushes six feet high."

Josh took another sandwich. "I imagine Phyllis was pretty badly worried over Jim," he said to Lucy.

Lucy told him how Phyllis had driven along the highway hoping Jim would come out there. "I went down to tell her you and Rich had gone back up for him."

"That make her feel better?"

"Oh, I'm sure it did."

"I wouldn't have gone if I hadn't felt she was going to

be frantic." He bit into his toast as though he were crashing through the brush on the mountain.

She looked at him, forcing him to meet her glance. "I think you were worried about him yourself."

"Well, I . . ." he waited as Lucy nodded at Ellie.

Then as she saw Ellie slipping out the door, she called, "Remember we're going to eat at five-thirty; it gets cold so early."

Josh brought out his glasses, shifting them in his hands. Sometimes she wished he did smoke. She watched the sun polish the smooth surface of the old pine table, remembering how Josh had bought the table at an auction and taken off the paint, rubbing it to this pale luster. Touching it, her hand always seemed to reach Josh.

"Of course I'm concerned about him," Josh said. "I made him angry up there on the mountain." He pushed his cup back and smoothed the curled corner of the place mat. "I finally told him he hadn't done what he had meant to; he had let himself get hung up in that place where he wasn't content and now, subconsciously, he was punishing himself by feeling guilty."

"Oh Josh! That couldn't be so."

"Of course it could. You don't know the force of a frustration like that. I just want to make him see this fool obsession of his for what it is."

After a moment, she asked, "What did Jim say?"

Josh got up and pushed in his chair. "He said he had to think about what I'd said, so he was going back by himself, and then he just walked off."

"Why didn't you go after him? You shouldn't have let him go off angry."

"He said things to me, too, Lucy, that I won't forget right away." Josh hesitated as though he were going to tell her, but instead he said, "I think I'll go up and sleep for an hour."

After he had gone, she went on sitting at the table. What was happening to them? They only wanted to help Jim and Phyllis, and instead they were . . . almost quarreling, saying things to hurt each other. Josh shouldn't have said that. . . .

She carried the dishes over to the sink, trying to joggle her mind free from her doubt, but it was held too firmly. Perhaps Josh didn't really understand Jim. She let down the drop leaf and pushed the table against the wall.

That night Phyllis could feel them all trying to make the dinner a "celebration," as Lucy had said. Josh's voice was overly jovial.

"This steak is a trifle better than munching hardtack and chocolate bars, the way you were doing last night," he said as he passed James's plate.

And she could hear James's tone matching his. "This is what I dreamed of after I got myself so gloriously lost. You'd have thought I was the original tenderfoot."

"Mom said you wouldn't get lost!" Harp jeered.

Ellie was quick to defend him. "He means just for a minute in the dark, silly!"

"No, Ellie," James said. "I was really lost up there. And I would have sworn I couldn't get lost on that mountain. It just goes to show that you don't know yourself very well." He seemed to be talking directly to Josh. Phyllis felt the simple remark vibrating in the air, like a tuning fork. Did everyone hear it, or was it just in her own mind that it seemed to make a special sound?

Then Josh said, "I suppose that's what you meant when you said yesterday that the only things we don't know about each other are what we don't know about ourselves."

"Something like that . . . I said 'understand,' I think; same thing."

"But you found your way out, remember." Josh's face seemed to change, to look almost eager, and his voice was warm, but Phyllis remembered the way he had looked in the study and turned away from him to James.

"Yes, but I saw quite a bit while I was thrashing around through that wilderness up there before I found my way out," James said slowly. The talk seemed to move so swiftly

135

from meaning nothing to meaning more than Phyllis could be sure of Josh didn't answer.

"It's a miracle you three didn't come down with pneumonia after a night like that," Lucy cut in.

Everything was just as it had been other nights when they had eaten together out here, Phyllis thought. Except that the maples along the drive kept up a constant hushing sound in the small August breeze, and sometimes the flames in the hurricane lamps waved against the globes. Fireflies flashed, more weakly than on hot summer nights, and katydids warned monotonously of frost. But she mustn't sit here like a mummy; she must say something, she thought uneasily.

"Did Rich's girl forgive him for standing her up?" she asked, trying to be humorous. It fell flat because Josh answered seriously.

"I don't know why he couldn't bring her up here for dinner tonight. He seemed to think they'd have a better time at a hamburger joint." They all would, Phyllis thought.

"We'll have a party some night soon for Rich's friends." Lucy intervened. "At their age, of course, they don't like family parties."

When James said he would drive Harp and Ellie in after dinner for the last band concert, Phyllis wanted to protest at being left with Josh and Lucy. Then Josh said he would go with James.

"And we'll wait and have our coffee when you come back," Lucy said.

But it was awkward with Lucy, too. Did Lucy feel that? Phyllis hardly knew what they said to each other. "Such a good steak . . . the best peaches we've had this summer." When Phyllis took the last dishes out to the kitchen, she lingered there, looking across the meadow at the dark outline of mountain where James had been lost. Josh had said, "I think you pushed him to the brink."

She stood in the doorway of the kitchen facing Lucy.

"Lucy, do you think I've been bad for James?"

Lucy went on arranging coffee cups on a tray. "I do think Jim must feel your anxiety often, because I can feel it. You're so wrapped up in him, Phyl, he never has to come out of his problems to find you. Do you know what I mean?"

"No, I'm afraid I don't," Phyllis said, angry suddenly at the sure hands moving the cups.

"I mean you're always sort of hovering. . . ." Lucy laughed to soften what she had said. "Oh, Phyl, please understand that Josh and I only want to help you both. You asked me, so I tried to tell you what I thought." She picked up the tray. "Let's go out and have a cup while we're waiting."

Phyllis felt herself sitting stiffly in the chair. She was aware of her hands lying heavy and useless in her lap, and with an effort reached for the cup Lucy held out to her. She was silent, just as she had been that other time. "Don't cling so hard to your father, Phyllis," Laura had said.

But that wasn't the same thing at all. She had been a child then. "You can love him more when you don't," Laura had said. But what did anyone know of anyone else? How did Lucy dare sit and criticize? She had no right.

Lucy's rocker rubbed against the house, and she jerked it forward. "These old rockers travel so," she said.

Phyllis took a swallow of coffee. Very well then, she had clung to James. But why shouldn't she? How else were you one in mind and spirit as well as body? And even now, what were they doing but waiting for Josh and James to come back; suspended, in a way. Women were like that.

"I'm going in to get a sweater," Lucy said. "Are you warm enough, or do you want to go in?"

"I'm fine."

"I'll take the coffee in so it will be hot for them."

It was a relief to have Lucy go, to sit alone in the dark and fold her arms around herself to keep warm. And now she could think about James and the way he had said, "I'd have found my way out eventually" when he was talking about being lost. Couldn't he mean that he had found his way out of feeling guilty?

The night quickened with the sound of the jeep coming up the drive.

"There they are!" Lucy called from the door of the kitchen. Phyllis leaned forward, no longer folding her arms around herself.

But the men went on sitting in the jeep after Josh turned off the ignition. The sound of their voices came up to the porch and then a long silence before they spoke again. Lucy brought out the coffeepot and set it on the table.

"Where are the . . ." she began, then stopped as she heard them talking in the jeep. "I'm going to call them in a minute," she said, but she waited. "Do you realize we don't hear the frogs any more in the evenings? I just noticed; only the katydids now."

"I guess that's so," Phyllis agreed.

They were coming now, their feet grating on the gravel.

"Hello," Lucy said. "We were just about to bring you coffee in the jeep."

"Curb service," James suggested.

But Josh was silent as he sat down and took his cup. Then he said, "Well, Lucy, I'm going to have more time around here. Jim doesn't think the world will suffer seriously if I don't finish my book."

"There will be a good many people disappointed if you don't," Lucy answered.

"You know, Joshua," James said, "you have a not altogether lovable habit of rephrasing remarks to suit yourself and interpreting them entirely out of context. What I said was that I'd rather see you write your book on Lucretius first. You can do this one when you've retired."

"You mean when I'm senile," Josh said.

The faint hushing sound in the trees was all that filled the moment's silence. Then the clamor of the katydids began, shrilling out their alarm.

"Don't be ridiculous, Josh!" Lucy said. Phyllis waited for James to say something. Didn't he see that he had hurt Josh?

"Since I don't seem to be able to follow the complicated workings of your mind, perhaps senility has already set in," Josh went on, as though no one but James were there.

"Nothing complicated about it," James muttered. "If

you could look at the thing for a minute as I see it. We went over all this on the mountain; let's not rake it up again."

No one spoke for a moment. Josh's spoon fell on the floor with a loud clatter, and as he reached down to pick it up, he said, "I hoped you might see things a little differently after you bolted off by yourself and had time to think about it."

"Bolted?" Phyllis tried to see James going off like that. What had they said to each other before?

"No," James said. "I feel the same way."

"Well, as I said before, Jim . . ." Phyllis felt the change in Josh's voice; it was impersonal, almost cold. "It's entirely up to you, but I hate to see you pass up a rather unusual opportunity. And I confess I can't for the life of me see what holds you there. You can go on feeling guilty here if you've got to."

James struck a match, letting it almost burn his fingers before he lit his cigarette, then he tossed the match absentmindedly on the stones. "Since I do feel . . . guilty . . . obsession or not, I don't care to use that boy as a means of bettering myself."

Josh's voice seemed to tighten. He leaned forward. "Let's be very clear about this, Jim; you mean you'd rather throw away a real opportunity so you can hug your precious fantasy all the tighter to you. Pick up that match. If you have to smoke, at least you don't have to make a mess."

Phyllis couldn't look at James, or at Josh or Lucy. She watched the maple leaves beyond the post light move; there was no other movement. She heard the hushing sound in the trees.

"Josh, for Heaven's sake! That's all right," Lucy said. "The children can sweep up here in the morning."

Phyllis flung herself out of her chair, brushing past Josh, and picked up the match from where it lay on the stones. She went quickly down the steps without a word, not stopping until she was out of reach of the light.

Perhaps Josh was James's friend who meant everything

to him; perhaps he said those things because he wanted to help . . . her mind curled in scorn over Lucy's words . . . but he could not speak to James that way. And he could not tell her she had caged James by her fears and worries, either. Now James would know what Josh was like, how cruel and unjust he could be.

And then she was crying against the tree in the orchard, with her face against the bark. What if Josh was right? And all the years that she and James had lived together, in some way she had not been conscious of, were blighted by her fears? Not the fears Josh said she had, about what people thought, or James's success in the school . . . Josh was so stupidly wrong about those. But that other fear that Josh didn't know, a fear that she was too . . . say the fat-cheeked word . . . too happy, so that she could never quite trust her joy. "You can bring a condition about by fear alone," Josh had said. Had she? Had she done that?

After a little, the rough bark hurt her face, and she stopped crying and went in to wait for James.

Lucy started to follow Phyllis. She mustn't go off like that. How could Josh have been so boorish! But there was nothing she could say. Josh would have to say something. She sat back and watched Phyllis's light dress until it was lost in the dark of the orchard. Josh hadn't moved since Phyllis had got up so swiftly. His face was in the dark, but she knew how it must look. As it did when he was angry with Rich—his mouth gathered up together in a crooked line, his eyes dark and moody, and his whole expression desolate, so that it went to her heart. She glanced over at Jim. He was rubbing out his cigarette in the ash tray. What was he thinking?

"Why didn't you throw something at him, Jim?" she asked. "You know, Josh, Phyl doesn't understand your joking and scolding about smoking. She thinks you insulted Jim. You ought to go and tell her . . ."

"I didn't happen to be joking," Josh said.

"I know you weren't," Jim answered.

140

Jim wasn't angry, Lucy thought, but there was a sadness in his voice that was worse. It was growing too cool to sit out here any longer, and yet the evening mustn't end like this.

"Whatever I say doesn't seem to make much difference to you, Jim," Josh said.

"You know it makes a great difference." Jim sounded as though he were going on, but he stood up. "You need to go to bed, boy; you must be dead." There, Lucy thought, Josh must feel the affection in Jim's voice.

But Josh only said, "I slept up there on the mountain. You didn't think I stayed awake worrying all night!"

"Thank goodness you two aren't off up there tonight," Lucy said. "Good night, Jim. Say good night to Phyl for me." Tell her, she wanted to add, tell her Josh didn't mean to sound like that, but she was silent.

"Good night, Josh," Jim said.

"Good night," Josh answered.

Their good nights were quickly lost in the sound of the maples. The coolness that had been creeping down from the wilderness of the mountain all evening had sharpened to cold.

"James!" Phyllis called when she heard the door open. She had not been asleep, only lying there, her mind swinging like a pendulum between Lucy's words, "I mean you're always sort of hovering," and Josh's, "Pick up that match . . . you don't have to make a mess." Back and forth, back and . . . no quiet rhythm of thought, but racketing crazily, held by the word "hovering" until it broke away wildly and banged against Josh's words.

"Hi, Phyl," James said from the other room, but she heard the scratch of his match and the creak of the reed chair as he sat down.

"James?" she called again. . . . "I mean you're always sort of hovering" . . . She wouldn't go in to him, only wait. . . . "Pick up that match" . . . But the pendulum stuck there until she burst out, "Why do you stay a minute longer, James? He's impossible!"

141

James came into the bedroom. "Oh, that doesn't matter, Phyl. Josh was just upset." He said it so mildly, wearily.

She sat up and turned on the light on the low table beside the bed. "Of course it matters. He can't talk to you like that!"

James began undressing without answering. His clothes, which he dropped on the old-fashioned spindle chair, seemed to fall in a meek pile. "I hate him," she said.

"No you don't, Phyl. You don't understand him," James said. "He thinks my feeling responsible for Leonard is just a way of punishing myself for not doing the kind of thing I meant to once. He won't believe that I liked what I was doing." James stood a moment, naked, staring out into the night. "I suppose it's that he's disappointed in me."

"He's disappointed in you!" she cried out.

But as though he hadn't heard her, he said, "I've known he felt this way . . . maybe that's partly why I wanted Leonard to do great things."

James's tone seemed to mock at himself, and his face looked haggard as he stood above the lamp to turn it off. She was glad when he came to lie beside her.

"James," she murmured against his head, "don't worry any more about Josh." No clinging . . . hovering; James reached out to her. Always again this quick catch of the breath, this closeness that shut out everyone else . . . the rest against James's shoulder. No need to talk.

James moved his arm. His voice seemed to come to her from a long way off. "If all Josh and I mean to each other can't make us understand . . . or take on faith what we can't . . . what good is it?"

She turned away from him, all sense of closeness, or safety, wiped out in a hopeless feeling of weariness and dull anger. Couldn't he ever forget Josh? Did he even remember that he had loved her? She could feel him going on with his own thoughts.

When he said "Good night, dear," she made no answer, and lay still, as though she were asleep, listening to his feet crossing the room.

142

Nineteen

THE NEXT MORNING, Lucy went down to the garden after breakfast. Josh had hardly said anything all through the meal. "Cheery little gathering!" Rich had said, in the way she minded most. And Ellie had raised her eyebrows and shaped the words "What's the matter with Dad?" silently with her lips. Lucy had said aloud, as though saying it would make it true, "Nothing is the matter, Ellie."

Josh had gone on into his study when he was through, and she had heard him typing as though he were working on his book. She was relieved but she wondered how he could put his mind on it. Her own was so jangled she had to get out of the house by herself.

The garden was full of summer, of yellow squash and polished peppers and corn tasseling, and the sun was warm on her back and arms, the way she liked it, but suddenly, kneeling by the tomato vines, she wished it were fall . . . and the garden bare and the earth frozen.

The first weekend in October, she and Josh would come up by themselves and be startled again by the way the leaves had fallen and the house loomed naked from the road. The mountain would have a few last flags of color, and the air would be as clear as . . . "as truth," her father used to say.

They would come to close the place for the winter, but they would put that off the first day and go for a long walk. The leaves would be piled thick along the stone wall and would smell of leaf mold and cold dirt, and when she laid her hand on the wall, the stone would be cold and rough. In the night, perhaps, a wind would blow against the gable of their bedroom, and if it was a high wind, it would thrash against the branches of the maples, and she would feel the strength of the old house. Nothing could shake it.

Her basket was full of corn and tomatoes, and as though that had been the reason she had filled it, she went down to take some to Phyllis. Should she say something about last night? She could tell her how Josh had said, "I didn't mean to blow up, but he's such a damn fool" . . . not the last part, of course . . . but she didn't want Phyllis to think she was apologizing for him. Better to let it go. People said hurting things when they cared so much; Phyllis must know that.

Once Lucy stepped out in the grass, summer brushed hot and dusty against her bare ankles.

Phyllis was sitting at the edge of the orchard, reading. With her head bowed over the book propped on her knees, she looked almost like a young girl. "Phyl!" Lucy called.

Phyllis went on reading, but she turned a page. Lucy was sure she had heard and was pretending not to. She started talking before she reached Phyllis so that there would be no terrible moment of awkwardness. The only thing to do was to assume that Phyllis wasn't still angry, that Jim had made things all right. Jim must understand. . . .

"I brought you some tomatoes. They're dead ripe. Try one. I think they're so good when you eat them right out of the garden." Lucy polished one with her skirt and handed it to Phyllis.

Phyllis looked up with just a little too much surprise, Lucy thought. Her voice was cool.

"Oh thank you. They smell so good."

"I brought some corn, too." They were both standing now, leaning over to eat the tomatoes so the juice could run down on the grass.

"They say it's going to be an early winter," Lucy said, making her voice suggest an old country woman's.

"How do they know?" Phyllis asked.

"Something about the thickness of the corn silk." Now Lucy wished she hadn't mentioned winter. "Well, I mustn't stand here gossiping if I'm going to get any weaving in."

Halfway across the orchard, she came back. "Weren't Harp and Ellie killing, sleeping in the cemetery last night?" Then she added, "It's been so good for Ellie to have Harp here this summer."

"So good for Harp, too," Phyllis answered. But Lucy felt, as she went back to the house, as though the simple statement had really said something else; that being here had not been good for Phyllis and Jim. She heard Phyllis calling and turned, but Phyllis was only saying thank you again.

She must not read meanings into casual remarks, Lucy told herself. She stopped to smooth the loose dirt of a mole-hill, but when she tamped it down with her foot, a hole was there.

She left the corn on the bench outside for Ellie to shuck for dinner. "And get all the silk out," she would say, just as her mother had used to say to her. Wasn't she growing more like her mother? She liked things in order now, too, and felt compelled to keep stamps in the little pillbox on the desk and all the keys labeled, as she had never used to do. She liked her days ordered, too. That was the trouble with this summer—it had been so disordered, so different from the way she had planned.

She knew now why her mother had seemed uninterested sometimes. She herself found it difficult to listen to Ellie's long thoughts when she was caught up in her own. When Josh was talking sometimes, she could feel detached . . . even now . . . for what had this uncomfortable tenseness to do with her? She was tired of thinking whether Josh was right or Jim was hurt or . . . She took the tomatoes into the house and held them under the water, wiping them gently so as not to bruise the thin, taut skin. It gave her an odd feeling to stop and think whether she had changed. Certainly she was not the same person who had married Josh that June day out on the lawn.

When were you most yourself? She must ask Jim and Phyl and Josh that question. When you were young, or growing into middle age, or when you were old? Did some people change . . . like Jim . . . and some people stay the same? If you began that train of thought, you began to feel the strangeness of yourself, of everyone. Who was Jim, or Phyl, or Josh, let alone yourself? And then you wondered if you really knew anyone. Even this house, which she had always loved, and this meadow and orchard and the mountain shimmered and became unreal as she stood there by the window. And this summer, already, was made up of snapshots pasted in one of the old albums in the bookcase, and the things that had happened were only half remembered.

She saw Josh way down in the meadow. He hadn't stayed long in the study. What was he doing down there? She watched him tying a strip of white cloth around the trunk of a tree. He was real and solid and knew what he was doing.

He was wearing an old shirt, faded on the shoulders. Now he was looking up into the tree, marking it for cutting, yet hating to cut it down, too. Josh loved trees the way her father had, each one on the place. He moved farther away and tied a piece of cloth around another tree. All summer he had been going to thin them out so they could get a better view from the house; the trees had grown so. But why would he do that now? In the fall, when they came up by themselves, as a reward for this hard summer, Josh could do it. He could get someone from the village to cut down the trees. But he had to be doing something, of course. She went outside and called. Josh turned and waved, and she went running down to him.

After Lucy left her, Phyllis stood holding the corn and tomatoes. "Thank you," she called again. She should have said something more . . . but she had nothing to say to Lucy, or to Josh either. All she could do was get through these next days until she and James could leave. She wished she could avoid seeing Josh again. But even when they were home, James would go on thinking about him . . . the way he had last night.

Her face was sober as she stripped off the pale-green sheath of cornhusk and picked out the cotton-coarse threads of silk. One thread persisted, clinging between the close-growing kernels of corn.

Could Josh be right? Even partly right . . . that somehow James felt guilty to . . . to punish himself for not doing what he meant to do? The green world of grass and leaves, yellowing at the edges, seemed to move crazily in front of her.

She tried to think back, to catch James's face when he came in or went out, in his groans over regulations and committees, and his interest in different students . . . not just that one boy. She forced her eyes to see him working with . . . Leonard. And when Leonard got the scholarship, she remembered how he had said, "You ought to see him, Phyl. He's like a boy with a ticket to the World Series!" Didn't that prove . . . How could you know these things for sure?

A door banged across the meadow. Phyllis stood up and saw Lucy coming down the stone steps. For a minute, she thought she was coming back, but Lucy went on down to talk to Josh. Phyllis didn't want them to see her if they came this way. Leaving the corn and tomatoes on the grass, she climbed the stone wall and started up the old road that had become so familiar, because she had fled up here so often. Wasn't she always fleeing . . . like last night? She should have stayed up there and said something to Josh. But she couldn't have said anything; she could only get up and leave.

"Mom!" Harp was coming behind her. "Where you going?"

"Oh, I thought I'd take a last walk up this road," she said, waiting for him.

He walked along beside her.

"You and Dad got haircuts this morning for the trip, didn't you?" she said. The line of paler skin at the edge of his hair seemed to suggest some inner quality usually covered over by the tan, she thought. "It's a good thing we're going, Harp, you're growing right out of all your jeans."

"Mom," Harp said, "do you want to go back?"

147

"Why, yes," she said quickly. "Don't you? Think how good it will be to get home."

He didn't answer because he was balancing on the extreme edge of the grassy bank above the road, and Phyllis began to picture the winter to herself. It would be like last winter, after all. James would go off to high school in the morning, and she would call to Harp to watch the street crossing, and at one she would go to the library . . . but they would be living their own lives again.

In her mind, she ran upstairs to their own bedroom and found the earrings she had forgotten and left on the dresser when they went away; she flung up a window, and the sound of the cars rushed in. In the bottom drawer of the desk downstairs was the newspaper clipping she had hidden there, not quite able to throw it away: BODY OF A YOUNG MAN . . .

Harp jumped down from the bank. "I like it here better," he said.

They turned in at the old cellar hole. Phyllis stood a minute on the doorstep, looking into the tangled growth of weeds, while Harp climbed down in. Next winter, Phyllis thought resentfully, they would keep remembering this summer, but it would be a long time before they could talk about it, and some things they would never speak of.

"Uncle Josh says I could build a house here sometime," Harp said, looking up at her with the plan of it already in his eyes.

"It's bigger than it looks," she said. "You'd have quite a job."

She would always wince when she thought of so many things that had happened this summer. But they had happened; they couldn't change them now. "Come on, Harp, we'll go as far as the old cemetery, then we must go back."

Harp went over to see the revolutionary soldier's grave in the far corner. "Lemuel Biddeford . . . first soldier in Lennox County to die for his country!" Harp's voice shrilled in excitement across the grass-grown peace of the graveyard.

Phyllis's eyes found the slate headstone of the boy drowned

148

at sea, remembering that she had fled even from here, crying over the boy . . . not the one drowned in 1841, but James's boy, Leonard. The tombstone in the old cemetery carried the headline, too, she thought wryly.

"Come, Harp! We have to go."

"He was nineteen, Mom," Harp said as he walked along beside her.

"Who was?"

"Lemuel Biddeford."

"Oh," Phyllis said.

"Why doesn't Dad want to stay here?" Harp asked suddenly. "Uncle Josh wants him to, and Ellie thinks it's mean that he doesn't."

It was hard to answer quickly. "We only came for the summer, Harp, and Dad has his own work to do. . . . There's Ellie waiting for us," she broke off to say.

"Uncle Jim and I've been to the village," Ellie announced.

"We went there this morning to get haircuts," Harp said. "Why did Dad go again?"

"We went to see some folks Uncle Jim used to know. You rode in the car, Harp, but we walked all the way. And, Aunt Phyllis, Uncle Jim invited me to go and we talked about Uncle Jim's school and my school and everything."

"That was fine," Phyllis said. Ellie always gave her information piecemeal, as though each detail had its own importance.

"Aunt Phyllis, I'm glad Uncle Jim let Raccy out, because he's different now. I mean, he doesn't feel so bad about the drowned boy."

Phyllis was startled. "Why do you say that, Ellie?"

"Because I can tell. Maybe he feels just as bad when he thinks about him, but . . ." She chewed the inside of her cheek in her effort to be exact. ". . . He isn't thinking about him all the time any more."

"Where is Uncle Jim now?" Phyllis asked.

"He and Dad are sitting on the wall, talking," Ellie said. "Beat you to the post light and back, Harp!"

Phyllis watched them going off across the meadow. How had Ellie happened to say that? Was it so? But when she saw James coming down from Josh's, she thought that Ellie didn't see the troubled look his face had, or how quiet had grown on him. It struck her suddenly that you would hardly speak of him as a young man, though he was.

"I hear you've had a wonderful walk to town," she began.

"Yes," James said. "Phyl, it's time to go. Maybe we should have gone sooner."

The whole late summer afternoon seemed to hang silent, holding the sadness of James's voice in its hollow.

"You mean go right now, James? Not wait till Friday?"

"Oh no, we'll go on Friday. I just mean that it's time we went."

Twenty

WHEN RICH CAME DOWNSTAIRS after dinner, Lucy said quickly, "Don't go to town tonight, Rich."

"I'm not. I'm going down to see Jim," Rich said. Lucy noticed that his head reached almost as close to the top of the door frame as Josh's did.

"Jim and Phyl are coming up in a few minutes. We're going to have a lovely evening by the fire."

"I want to see him first." Rich said it so ominously. Now what was the matter? Lucy watched the way the firelight caught a light streak in his hair, and gave his face a glow, almost a spiritual look . . . like a young knight. Then he hunched his shoulder up so that he could rub his chin against it in a perfectly grotesque way. "I want to get Jim to talk to Dad about my not going back to college this fall."

His eyes caught hers, looking to see how she was taking it, and then moved back to the fire. She wouldn't rise to his remark.

"Don't be absurd, Rich. Just because you had that one condition. . . ."

"That isn't it. Jim says I'd have to go down and take the exam and pass off the condition anyway."

Jim! What did Jim have to do with it? "I would think you would talk to Dad before you consulted Jim."

"I know what Dad'll say. He'll try to snow me with fifty-one reasons why I should go back, and tell me how disappointed he'd be."

Her voice was quiet. "He would be very much disappointed."

"Yeah, but he wouldn't really listen. At least Jim sees my point."

Why did Rich affect that sloppy way of speaking when he was embarrassed? It was so unattractive. She couldn't see his face because he bent over and retied his shoelace.

"You know Dad always listens to you, but, Rich, wait till Jim and Phyllis go before you talk to him about this idea of yours, will you?"

"But I'd kinda like to tell Dad now. You're always so afraid of some kind of a blowup! Anyway, I want to see Jim first." He went out, banging the kitchen door after him. On the pine boards, where he had been standing, Lucy noticed the imprint of his rubber soles, three interlocking circles.

Of course, he was just talking, but it would bother Josh, and she did mind a "blowup" just now. Josh had dealt with plenty of boys who wanted to drop out in the middle of college; frantic parents were always calling him up, and Josh calmed them, but this was a little different. And if Jim took Rich's side . . .

She picked up the hearth broom and swept some fragments of bark inside the screen. There were the initials cut in the corners. She and Jim and Josh had spent most of a winter's afternoon at it, years ago, using a hammer and a screw driver, she remembered. The shallow-cut lines had lasted all this time: a large J with a small B and C flanking it to stand for both Jim and Josh: Jim Cutler, Joshua Blair; and in the other corner, her own initials, L.S.H., Lucy Stone Hastings.

She hung the broom back on its hook and stood a moment with her hands on the high mantel, looking into the fire. They had too much behind them, she and Jim and Josh, to let anything spoil it now. She laid another log on the fire to make it blaze higher, and brought from the dining room the pitcher of red leaves that the children had picked today.

Harp came in ahead of the others, and she put her arm around his shoulders. "Would you like to make some popcorn, Harp?"

152

"Sure, Aunt Lucy," he said, but she felt him still cautious, remembering the paint episode.

"My, we're going to miss you around here, Harp. I don't know what Ellie will do without you."

But, of course, it was one of those fatuous remarks only adults stoop to answer. "Have you had fun here, Harp, this summer?" she asked suddenly, wishing for a moment that Rich were Harp's age again.

"Lotta fun," Harp answered, one hand rubbing the knob on the chair back.

"Good!" she said in a tone of voice that let him go. "You know where to find the popper, and the corn is on the top shelf of the cupboard." She wondered what Harp would remember from this summer; how he would remember her. What had he done with the boat he was painting when he spilled the paint? She didn't believe she had ever seen it. Ellie would know. She couldn't ask Harp.

Josh asked as soon as he came in, "Jim and Phyl coming up? This is a good night for a fire. At the store they were saying it's going to frost."

"Of course they're coming. Did you get the chain saw?"

"No. I decided we'd use the old cross-cut saw. Jim and Rich and I can trade off. I thought we could go it together."

She could see that he liked the idea of their working together instead of one man ripping away with the power saw, but she said, "It'll take you lots longer. Have you explained your project to Jim?" Her tone was carefully teasing.

"Jim won't mind. Rich may grumble. He'd like to run the chain saw by himself." Then he said, "I wish Jim weren't leaving so soon."

Why did he say that? Surely he couldn't still hope to change Jim's mind. It was better that Jim leave now. Rich leaned too heavily on him. She thought for a moment of telling Josh what Rich had said. Then she remembered what Ellie had said tonight, drying dishes; it might make him feel better.

"Josh, Ellie said an amazing thing tonight. She said,

'Uncle Jim's felt better about that drowned boy ever since he let Raccy out.' I asked her what made her say that, and she just said that she could tell. And you know, Josh, the child is perceptive."

She could feel his interest, almost eagerness, but before she could say any more, she heard steps on the porch and hurried to fling open the door.

Phyllis wore that deep-blue scarf tucked into the neck of her sweater, and Lucy had a swift, childish satisfaction that she was weaving the new pattern now. Jim was smoking a cigarette, but he threw it into the fire as he came in. It was irritating, the way he went on smoking. Rich came in with them.

"Do you know it must be down to forty?" Jim announced. "I told Phyl she may yet see what it's like up here in winter."

Lucy was glad when Jim sat over on the shabby old leather couch where she had seen him so many times years ago. Josh took the Morris chair.

"Sit over here, Phyl; this old rocker is the most comfortable chair in the room," Lucy urged.

"Oh, I like this hassock near the fire for a bit," Phyllis said, holding out her hands to the fire as though in proof. The firelight seemed to polish her smooth straight hair and give a little color to her pale face. Lucy noticed that she hardly looked at Josh.

"Well, then, I'll take it, and feel like the mother of you all," Lucy said.

Ellie came in with a bowl for popcorn, and the popping of the corn and the danger of spilling the butter in the three-legged firkin kept the idle conversation together. The children had big glasses of milk, and Josh brought beer for the rest.

"Rich," Josh said, "Jim suggests that you deserve beer tonight to celebrate your finishing up your physics. I'll give it to you in the pewter stein."

Rich flushed as he took it, and glanced over at Jim. "Thanks," he said, standing by the fireplace to drink it.

154

"There!" Lucy wanted to say to him, "you see how Dad is." She wished Josh hadn't said that Jim suggested it. Oh, now everything was going to be all right. They might have posed for an advertisement on the back of some magazine. What were the people in the pictured ad always laughing about?

"J. C.," Josh began, bringing up the old nickname almost as though he had looked at the carved initials tonight, "I hate to tell you, but I've got a project for tomorrow that I'll need your help with."

"I suspected it when you used my initials," Jim retorted.

"All summer," Josh went on, "I've been going to clear out enough trees and branches so we could have a clearer view of the mountain, and unless I do it while you're still here to help me, I won't get it done; I'm sure of that."

"Wait a minute, wait a minute!" Jim protested.

This was the way it used to be. "My, this is good popcorn, Ellie and Harp!" Lucy said.

"Can we sleep out on the porch in our sleeping bags tonight, Mother?" Ellie asked.

"On a night like this! For a person who has a perfectly good bedroom and a bed to herself, Ellie, you're strangely loath to sleep in it," she objected mildly, knowing that it made the permission more valuable.

"No taking off for the cemetery tonight, young man," Josh said to Harp.

"No sir," Harp answered, giggling.

Lucy met Phyllis's eyes and smiled. "I do think they've had a wonderful time this summer," she said, feeling that she was repeating herself, half waiting for Phyllis to say they all had.

"Harp is going to complain bitterly when he has to sleep in the house at home," Phyllis said.

"I had a cordial note from Hopkins, Josh." Jim took a letter out of his pocket. "I thought you might like to see it."

"Yes, I would." Lucy could catch the rasp in Josh's

155

tone. He did so hate to give up. "You still feel that you've got to devote your life to explaining to a lot of adolescents why a stone sinks when you throw it in a pond, I suppose?"

"It's rather an interesting thing to explain," Jim said. "And at least it's one thing I know the answer to."

"Bring your letter, Jim, and come on in the study," Josh said.

"Here, take some popcorn with you," Lucy said, filling one of the bowls to give Josh.

"Jim!" Rich said sharply as Jim stood up. His voice was taut with a meaning Lucy felt she understood. He was hacking at the fire with the poker.

"Oh no, Rich," Jim answered. "That's up to you." But Lucy could feel the warmth of his smile as he looked across the room at Rich . . . more than that—there was a kind of understanding that she minded, suddenly.

"Put on a record for us, will you, Rich?" she said. "The Chopin there on top."

Rich went over to the victrola. "These records are so old," he muttered. "You and Dad ought to get some new ones." Then he went on upstairs.

The notes of the concerto fell precise and whole into the uneasy quiet of the room. Phyllis left the hassock and took Jim's place on the old couch. Lucy picked up her knitting and went back to the rocker. Phyllis sat there so quietly, she wanted to say something to reach her.

"I think the summer has done a great deal for Jim, Phyl; don't you feel that?" She wondered whether she should tell her what Ellie had said, or would Phyllis mind Ellie's being so aware of Jim's moods?

Phyllis stirred, as though the question moved her. "Yes," she said slowly. "It's given him time to get some things worked out in his mind."

"It"? Some impersonal matter of time, not anything Josh had done. After all, he . . . both of them . . . had given up their summer to Jim and Phyllis. It hadn't been altogether easy, and Josh hadn't been able to finish his

156

book. He was perhaps too upset now to want to do it at all. Anger ran over her mind and then was gone. She remembered, almost with surprise, how eager they had been to have Phyllis and Jim come, how anxious to help them. "We only wish we could have done more. You know that, Phyllis."

"You have done a great deal," Phyllis said, but her words had a stiff sound in Lucy's ears.

Lucy was a little slow in taking off the record when it was finished, and it still revolved with an irritating insistence.

"As time goes on, Jim will get the whole miserable memory out of his mind, don't you think?"

"No," Phyllis said, unexpectedly. "I don't believe he ever will. That's what I'm coming to understand. When I called Josh so frantically, I thought that if James could just talk with Josh he would stop feeling responsible. But Josh couldn't do that for him." She was fingering the scarf at her neck when Lucy glanced over at her, and her eyes held Lucy's. "Some things, if they hurt enough, are always going to be buried in your mind, I think, so that all your thoughts have to . . . to grow out of their dust." She laughed uneasily. "That was certainly a poetic flight."

Lucy turned the record and stood by the player waiting for the first impersonal notes. Did Phyllis mean that things had hurt her here this summer, that she would never forget them? Or was she just thinking about Jim? If they hadn't come, it would have been so much better for Josh, maybe for Rich, too. Lucy's eyes sought the familiar objects of the room in discomfort at her own thought: the chairs that showed how long they had been sat in, the copper pitcher, the plaster replica of the Winged Victory, and the 1847 map of Vermont, relics of her father's and mother's living rather than her own, left as they were to preserve that living. She looked along the backs of the old books as though to protect them from what they were hearing. They were no more used to unpleasantness than she was. Of course, Phyllis was right in a way; some things that hurt were always there, but you didn't have to think of them. Like death. You decided not to think about it. When the summer was over, she would forget all the unpleasant things that had happened.

"You don't dwell on them, though," Lucy said. "You go on to other things."

"But they color the other things," Phyllis answered, and her face seemed stern to Lucy. "They change you."

"I suppose they do in a way, but the important things don't change, like love and the beauty of this country, and . . . and friendship." Lucy felt the truth seeping away from her words, leaving them sentimental.

"If the people change, they can't help changing toward each other," Phyllis insisted. "Isn't your marriage different from the way it was in the beginning?"

Phyllis asked it almost . . . defensively. What a question! "Deeper, that's all," Lucy said to the room as well as to Phyllis, who seemed lost in watching the fire. Perhaps this trouble of Jim's had made a difference to Phyllis and Jim. But if such a thing had happened to Josh, he would have brought it to her. She would have known how to help him. Phyllis should have been able to help Jim. And, anyway, Josh would have seen . . .

Rich pounded down the stairs and looked in from the hall.

"Mother, I've thought it over, and I am going to talk to Dad now."

"I wish you wouldn't. Dad and Jim have so little time left to be together."

After a moment's hesitation, Rich went on. They heard him knock at the study door, and Josh calling "Come in."

"Rich wants to stay out of college this year," Lucy explained to Phyllis.

"That would be too bad," Phyllis said, but too mildly, Lucy felt.

"It certainly would. He said he and Jim had talked about it."

"James hasn't said anything. Rich is such a fine boy, Lucy. James is so fond of him; we both are."

Lucy was pleased, but she said, "He's never been so

difficult as he has this summer." She added hastily, "I suppose he's at that age."

Once, the door of the study opened, and they heard Josh say, "Come back and sit down here, Rich. I know the way you feel; you're not unique. . . ." The door closed again, but not before they heard Rich's voice, lighter and a little strained, saying, "You don't listen to me, Dad. You just think of all the other boys you've talked to. Jim, tell him why I want to do this."

Lucy got up restlessly, and went over to put another log on the fire. But just as she dropped it on the andirons, she snatched it back, and peeled off the outer white bark. "I'll save this part, anyway; I always feel the white birch logs are too beautiful to burn."

When the men came out of the study, Josh's tone was humorous. "I'll tell you, Rich, tomorrow you can put in a good day chopping down trees and see how you'd like to spend a year as a lumberjack. We might be able to get you a job with Clem Greene."

"I wouldn't mind it," Rich said, and Lucy noticed that he went on up to his room. She looked at Josh questioningly.

"Just kidding a little," Josh said. "I'll tell you about it later. How about another beer, Jim?" Then he called from the kitchen, "Anyone rather have coffee? There is some. How about you, Phyl, you're the coffee drinker."

"Yes, I'll have coffee. Thanks, Josh," Phyllis said.

"Isn't that a grand old fireplace, Phyl?" Jim said, sitting back in the old Morris chair. "It's so tall you can see the whole height of the flame."

When he came back in, Josh sat down by Phyllis on the couch, and Lucy saw that Phyllis was smiling at something he said. How could she hold any grievance against Josh?

They watched the birch log burn to red, and Jim added one more log. "That's to hold the fire for the night."

"Remember the night we were so tired from skiing that we fell asleep here just as we were?" Josh asked.

"And your mother came and covered us with blankets in the night, Lucy," Jim remembered.

She did remember that time. She remembered waking in

the cold light of early morning, and creeping upstairs to bed. The fire had burned all the way out, and in the night the wind had blown white ashes out on the hearth. It had been horrid to be the only one awake.

"Well, we can't do that tonight if we're going to be on hand for your wood-chopping orgy tomorrow," Jim said. "Here, Josh, I want to give you back this agate before I go off with it. Rich gave it to you, I know."

"A lot of good it did you," Josh muttered.

"Oh, you can't tell. I do smoke less, you know. I might even stop some time."

Josh was standing by the dresser taking things out of his pockets when Lucy came upstairs. The agate made a small scratching sound as he laid it on the old marble top.

"Rich dropped a nice little bombshell tonight," Josh said. "He wants to stay out of college a year."

She wondered if Josh was really worried or only annoyed, but she said calmly, "He told me that, but he was just talking, I'm sure."

"He seems to have done quite a little talking to Jim. He came into the study and said he'd like to tell me something while Jim was there, because Jim understood how he felt. The inference was, of course, that I wouldn't."

"Lovely!" she said, so Josh would be amused, too, at the absurdity of it.

"Then he got off all this stuff about feeling he was immature, and wanting to be sure why he was studying. . . ."

"What did Jim say?"

"He didn't say anything till Rich was all through and then I asked him what he thought. He said those were all good reasons, worth listening to, but there were other reasons against it. It would have been considerably more help if he'd told Rich the very first time he brought up the question how foolish he'd be to waste a year now."

Josh sat on the bed without undressing.

"Oh, well, Josh, he was just being tactful for Rich's sake." She unbraided her hair and let the comforting weight of it fall down her back.

"Yes." Josh's tone grated. "So tactful he let Rich play around with the idea until he got it firmly planted in his mind. I told Rich in no uncertain terms that he'd have to finish college before he took a year out being a bum, or a beatnik, or whatever it is he has on his mind."

"All of you seemed in good spirits when you came out to the living room," Lucy insisted.

"You saw that Rich didn't stay around long. I don't know whether he's convinced or not."

"We had a good evening, though," Lucy said. Josh was worried about Rich, but after Jim and Phyllis left, they could make Rich see . . .

Josh ignored her remark. "Do you know what Jim said in the study, Lucy, before Rich burst in? He said if he came to me and said he had a hopeless disease, I wouldn't be able to help him face it; I'd just explain to him my theory as to why he got sick in the first place. Because if I accepted it, it would somehow attack my own health. He said you couldn't help a person that way." Josh seemed to be telling Jim's words to himself rather than to her.

Lucy finished brushing her hair and tied a cherry-colored ribbon around it for the night. "In the first place, there's no parallel," she said slowly, "and in the second place, I don't see what he means. Do you understand what he means, Josh?"

It took him several minutes to answer. "Well, it's obvious that he doesn't think I've done anything for him."

"But Josh, you have!"

"I'm beginning to wonder," Josh said slowly, "if, perhaps, Jim *did* push that boy too far. He's . . ."

She waited for him to finish. Was he going to say he could see how Jim might have been guilty? She had certainly felt tonight that Rich would do whatever Jim said about college. Boys were like that with Josh, too, of course. Josh didn't go on, and she wondered what he was thinking.

If he believed that about Jim, he must wonder about himself. That was what Jim must have meant about attacking his own health. A doubt like that was a kind of sickness, making you unsure of yourself. She crossed the room and pulled the curtains over the high windows, which she left open, sometimes, so they could see the sky; but it was too cold tonight.

Josh said finally, "Jim's not the same person I used to know."

"At least he knows you haven't changed . . ." She had meant to say, "in the way you feel about him," but Josh burst out impatiently.

"Of course I haven't." Then the irritation went out of his face and left it sad.

"Josh," Lucy said, "we only have one more day with them. You can't do any more for Jim than you have already. Don't argue with him, will you? Let's make it a pleasant day we can remember."

"There is nothing to argue with him about," Josh said. "We've come to that point."

It was that cup of coffee that kept her awake, Phyllis told herself as she turned restlessly in bed. She hadn't really wanted it, but it had been so surprising to hear Josh call her Phyl in that warm tone of voice. "How about you, Phyl?" he had called from the kitchen.

The orchard was less dark now, and she could make out the leaves. When the leaves were gone, the bare branches must claw at the sky like the illustrations in that red fairy-tale book that sometimes frightened small children in the library. As they looked at them, the branches became fingers and hands, all moving in the wind. When the trees out there in the orchard were weighed down by snow, they must look like huge toadstools. Thank goodness, she wouldn't be here.

That first morning, it had seemed so wonderful to look out into an orchard from her bed. She had been so grateful to be here. Now she only wanted to leave.

They would never come back again. But Lucy and Josh would talk about their coming back another summer. And she and James would say how they would love it. How much better it would be to say honestly, "No, we will not come back, and you would not want us to." There was some dignity in speaking the truth, even though it was unpleasant. But you didn't do that. You had to pretend you had had a splendid time. They would all act tomorrow . . . no, it was already today . . . as though they hated to have this the last day. But Lucy was anxious to have them gone and have the guesthouse empty. She wished she could tell Lucy that she knew how she felt, knew how much she had given up for them this summer. But she couldn't.

Josh would be relieved to have them gone, too. Even James had become a burden to him, keeping him from his book, wearing on him.

Last night, sitting in front of the fire, they had talked about the old days because they had come to a kind of dead end. When she and James first came, she had loved to hear them, and wished she had been a part of those times, but now it seemed almost pathetic to her, even boring. Lucy talked about what fun James used to be in college; how merry . . . as though he had changed and wasn't any more . . . as though the boy in him had died. Well, he wasn't a boy any more.

But why had she said all that to Lucy about things changing you? How could she ever have asked Lucy about her feeling for Josh? She buried her face in the pillow. How crude it must have sounded. And Lucy had moved so far away and her voice had been so polite and cool. Oh, would she ever learn not to burst out with questions like that! Never to be serious.

Lucy must think . . . Lucy would tell Josh, and he would blame her all the more for James's troubles. When Josh had come over and sat down by her on the couch tonight . . . last night . . . she had thought he might be going to say something about the time in the study, to try to explain . . . but he had only talked about what good friends Ellie and Harp were, and how much James had done for Rich.

Phyllis raised herself on one elbow so she could see James asleep. It was good to be the one who couldn't sleep, anyway. The room was cold, and she lay down again. Lucy had brought down an electric heater yesterday, but she

163

wouldn't use it. She couldn't bear to cost them any more. They could never repay Josh and Lucy as it was.

She had never taken so much from anyone before. She couldn't stand to be beholden. An ugly, old-fashioned word her mother had used long ago. "I don't want to be beholden to your father."

But it wasn't the money cost; they had spoiled Lucy's and Josh's summer. Phyllis squirmed into a smaller space and stared into the side of the room that was away from the window. But they hadn't meant to. They hadn't known how it would be.

They would go away now, and after she got home, she would write and try to thank Lucy. But what could she say?

Dear Lucy and Josh, I can't begin to tell you how much James and I appreciate . . . You were so good to open your arms and hearts . . . at a time when we were worried and disturbed. . . . (But you blamed me for my worry.)

She began again: We want you to know how deeply we appreciate . . . all you did for us. (That was better.) We never meant to ask so much or be a drag on your summer. (No, cross out the last part. That wasn't a thing you could say.) We shall never forget this summer with you in the little house by the orchard. (Never, never. Somehow it sounded cute. Better to take out "little.") We came back greatly refreshed. . . . (That wasn't the right word. They were going back tired and sad, but knowing more, maybe.) We have a new perspective. (That was true enough, but it could be taken so many ways.)

She gave it up and pushed back the covers so the chill struck at her throat and shoulders. It would have been so much better if they had never come, if she had never thought of calling Josh. Josh hadn't been able to lift James's feeling of guilt. He hadn't even been able to understand how he felt. James was just as alone as before . . . more so, because he and Josh couldn't talk to each other any more.

She would tell James now all those terrible things Josh had said, and how she writhed to feel beholden to Josh and

Lucy. You could only take kindness from people when . . . when could you? "I hate it," she whispered. Why shouldn't she tell James how she felt? Josh and Lucy had made her feel guilty if she worried James about anything.

She threw off the blanket as though it were the whole burden of her thoughts. The floor was cold under her bare feet. When she took a step, the boards creaked.

"It would be a different kind of world if anything really happened between us," James had said that time when he came down from the mountain.

Yes, but it had happened already.

Still . . .

She got back into bed, and pulled the covers up on her shoulders. She watched the leaves outside, in the green shadows of the orchard, move in a shiver of wind.

Twenty-one

"ALL WE NEED is a few more people here to look like a Brueghel painting," Lucy said to Phyllis. "The men sawing down trees, the harvest table, the children. Isn't this the pastoral scene for you!"

"Or a Grandma Moses Vermont lumber scene," Phyllis said. "I never expected to be part of one. Harp," she called, "don't get so close to Rich when he's chopping."

They were standing on the flagstones by the red-check-covered table. Josh and James had already felled one tree, working with the crosscut saw. Rich was chopping it up while Harp and Ellie dragged off the brush.

Josh was right, of course, Lucy thought. All this activity was just what they needed to drive away any megrims from this last day. And there was nothing Josh enjoyed so much as this, to have everyone doing something together. She could hear it in his voice.

"All right, now, Jim. You're not in training. Let Rich spell you."

Oh yes, this was good. And was there any place anywhere so absolutely perfect! The air was so clear, "clear as truth," but her father's words seemed somehow overblown.

"Did you ever see such a day, Phyl?" Lucy had a sense of giving, surrounding Phyllis with this loveliness of air and mountain and serenity.

Phyllis smiled as she received it. "It's beautiful."

"You just can't have a care in the world a day like this," Lucy said. Perhaps she shouldn't have pushed it.

"No," Phyllis said. "Not one. Though maybe I should go down and finish packing."

"Heavens no! You can do it this afternoon."

166

Ellie came up importantly to get a pail of water to carry down to the men, and it struck Lucy that she was unusually sober. Maybe she and Harp were not getting on.

"TIMBER!" Josh roared out.

"Timber!" Rich called after him, and Harp and Ellie joined in. The sound was echoed back as a slender elm fell across the meadow.

Then Lucy saw that the corner of the guesthouse was visible now from here. Had Josh noticed? He should have taken the next one. But even that did not matter today. "Of course, really, I think some judicious pruning would do as much, and they wouldn't need to take down the whole tree, but that's not as much fun," Lucy said, smiling at Phyllis. Did Phyllis see? This was the way Josh was sometimes. You had to understand. Surely she wasn't still hurt. "I'm going in to look at the beans. Why don't you stretch out there in the sun, Phyl?"

"All right, for a few minutes," Phyllis said. She lay back in the chaise and closed her eyes. She looked tired, Lucy thought, and felt a wave of pity. How could Phyllis bear to leave all this just now? She and Josh and the children would have another two weeks. No, Josh and Rich would have to go down next week for Rich's examination, but she and Ellie would be here.

"That's enough, Hercules! Time for a fresh horse," Jim shouted at Josh. It was good to hear them, she thought, as she went into the kitchen.

She wanted to say something to Jim before he left; to make sure he hadn't really changed . . . make him sure. For, of course, they hadn't really, any of them.

As she opened the oven door and took the cover off the bean crock, steam rushed out at her with the rich mingled smell of molasses and brown sugar and pork. She could leave the cover off now. She closed the big iron door of the oven, and the sound fell into the memory of it waiting in her mind. She must have been only a couple of years old when she first heard her grandmother close the oven door. It always seemed surprising that she could make it sound the same way.

When she turned around, Ellie was sitting at the kitchen table with her chin on her hand.

"Why, Ellie, I thought you and Harp were helping clear away the brush."

"Rich is horrid bossy and said to keep out of the way, and Harp's trying to finish *The Three Musketeers* before tomorrow. Besides, there isn't anything to do."

"On this wonderful day, there isn't anything to do!" Lucy began, and then, seeing how droopy Ellie was, said brightly, "Do you know what we're going to have for dinner?"

"I don't care what we're going to have. Anyway, I know, beans."

"That isn't all. We're going to have chocolate cake, and I saved the frosting bowl for you and Harp."

Ellie shook her head. "Harp can have it." One cheek and the corner of her mouth were pushed out of shape by her hand. Her hair had escaped the usual neat rolls and hung down around her face. She was close to tears.

Lucy sat down beside her. "Ellie."

Ellie buried her face in her arms on the table. "It won't be any fun when they're gone" came jerkily through her sobs. "I don't want them to go."

"I know, Ellie, but they don't go until tomorrow. You mustn't waste this lovely day."

"It isn't a lovely day."

"Ellie, that's very selfish. They only have one more day here, and you're going to spoil it for them." Sometimes, if she took a firm tone with Ellie . . . "Now go get your brush and comb, and I'll braid your hair, and we'll go out and see how they're coming."

Ellie sucked back her sobs and rubbed her arm over her face. She found her sandal under the table, then she went. Lucy sat waiting for her. There was no point in husking the corn till the last minute. Sweet corn with baked beans was a strange combination, but Jim and Phyl wouldn't get any like this after they left here, and Josh wanted them to have it once more. She wanted to tell Jim that Josh . . . it was hard to put it into words.

After Ellie's hair was combed and her face washed, they went outside. Phyllis must have gone on down to pack, after all. The men were sawing the old yellow birch Josh had talked of taking down for the last two years. That would really give them a far view. Then Lucy's eye landed on the abandoned cage under the porch stair.

"Ellie, do you want to earn a quarter? If you'll get Harp to help you clean out that cage and take it down, I'll pay you each a quarter. It's disgraceful that Rich has left it all this time." Ellie chewed at the inside of her cheek. If she kept that up, she would ruin the shape of her mouth. "I think it would be fine to get it out of the way so it won't remind Uncle Jim that he didn't fasten the cage tight, don't you?" Ellie looked at her solemnly and stopped chewing her cheek.

"But, Mother, he wanted Raccy to get out."

"All right, Ellie, but he doesn't want to be reminded of it now. Besides, it looks messy that way. Run tell Harp to help. He can take his book with him if he doesn't finish it. Ask him to bring a hammer and screw driver. And see how neatly you can roll up the chicken wire."

Ellie started, but stopped again. "What if we find another raccoon?"

"You wouldn't want to, would you, when you know Uncle Jim doesn't like to see them caged?" She hadn't meant to say so much about Jim. Ellie went on without answering.

They must never put any animal so close to the house again, Lucy thought, remembering those frantic scrabbling sounds the raccoon had made. They were enough to drive you crazy. She walked down to tell the men it was time to stop for dinner.

"Lucy, isn't this the darndest Yankee trick you ever heard of, getting me to saw wood for my keep?" Jim called out.

"It makes me blush for him, Jim," she said. "I don't know why you do it."

"Why, he loves it. He's having the time of his life," Josh protested. "How does it look now from the house?"

"Fine. It's going to be much better." She wouldn't tell him you could see the guesthouse from the porch now. "This is all you'll need to cut down, isn't it?"

"This is all I marked," Josh said. "When this one comes down, we really ought to be able to get a clear view. After all, you're interested in optics, Jim."

"You had to think hard to work that in," Jim retorted in good humor.

It was fine, too, sitting around the table at high noon, Lucy thought: she and Josh and their old and dearest friend, Jim, and his wife, and their children, sitting here in the sun on the last day of August. Today the air was so clear their voices had a special clarity about them. Phyllis said she had never realized what an echo there was until she heard them calling "Timber."

"Listen to it," Josh said. "More corn, Phyl?" he shouted, and the echo came back. "Corn, Phyl."

"You wretch," Phyllis said. "You counted."

"Do you remember how we used to stand here and shout out our names, and when your name came back, you wondered who that person really was?" Jim said.

How wonderful it was that, after all, they were ending this way, Lucy thought. It hadn't seemed possible to get back to this place. If they were just starting the summer again . . . or was it that they all knew the summer was ending?

She saw Ellie exchanging glances with Harp, and then they asked to be excused and started to slip away from the table.

"Ellie, come here a moment. Don't work on the hutch till we're through," she murmured to her.

"I know," Ellie answered, tossing her head.

"You think of me next week, Jim," Rich said. "When I take my exam." And, in an instant, they were all catapulted into the next month. She would still be here, thank goodness, Lucy thought for the second time today. But the summer would be gone. Another summer.

A moment ago she had been so pleased with all of them,

but now a sense of dissatisfaction bored into her pleasure. Why was it?

Jim passed his plate for another piece of cake. "Lucy, you made the cake I used to get your mother to make!"

"But certainly." There. That had said something to him. But why couldn't they say in words anything that mattered? Why couldn't they really talk together? Not the way Josh and Jim had talked, hurting each other, telling each other what was wrong, but listening to each other. If Josh could only say to Jim, "Maybe you're right" . . . because maybe he *was* right about going back there. Now that Josh understood how Jim could be responsible, partly anyway, if he could just say that to Jim. If he could even say that maybe he himself had . . .

Josh walked over to the center of the flagstones to get the whole long view. "Well, when we finish you'll be able to sit right here and see the whole mountain."

"Sure can, both sides of it," Jim said. "The side you came down and the one I came down."

"Well, boys," Josh said, but there was an effort in his heartiness, she felt.

"Joshua Blair, Jim isn't going to work all the last afternoon he's here," she broke in.

"I don't intend him to. We'll just get that baby down and then we'll leave it for Rich and me to saw up. As a matter of fact, I may hire Clem Green to come and saw it up this winter." They went off, and she heard Jim ribbing him about having the sawing done for him.

"You didn't stay long up here in the sun this morning," Lucy said to Phyllis. "I was so pleased when I thought you were going to fall asleep there."

"I did for a few minutes, but I finally stirred myself and went down to pack. I don't know how we brought so many things, but, of course, the trouble really is that you and Josh are sending us back with so much: apples and squash and potatoes, even Harp's Halloween pumpkin."

"You've been to Grandmother's in the country, you know," Lucy said. "Why don't you finish and come back up here?"

"Do you know what I'd really like to do?" Phyllis asked with sudden animation. "I'd like to go swimming again in the Quarry Hole."

"Of course. Josh and Jim will be ready by then, too." Lucy could see them all crowded into the jeep, careening down the hill from the Quarry, even singing. "Let's finish the coffee before we move. It's not exactly hot, but it tastes good."

"Sun-warmed," Phyllis said, smiling.

Phyllis was certainly less tied up in knots than she had been last night, Lucy thought. "Weren't we lucky to have such a good day?" Had she said that before? She felt as though she had. "Phyl, I wondered if you'd like those yellow mats I wove?" she asked, and was surprised at herself.

"Why, Lucy, I . . ."

Phyllis seemed so hesitant that Lucy said quickly, "I don't know whether you use mats or not. . . ."

"Oh yes, I do. Only I hate to have you give them away after all that work. You've done so much for us already."

The sound of hammering came up to them. Then Ellie and Harp went past the porch carrying a roll of chicken wire.

"Harp, what on earth are you doing?" Phyllis called.

"Something Aunt Lucy told us to do," he said.

"I asked them to clear out that hutch under the stair. It should have been done long ago," Lucy explained.

Ellie perched on the arm of the chair. "The cage is all gone," she announced. "But I know a better place to build one next time."

Phyllis brought her cup back to the table. "That must have been quite a job," she said.

"TIMBER!" Josh called, and Rich repeated it.

They hadn't quite let the tree fall where it would. They had it roped, but still the sound shattered the quiet of the valley; first the wrench and break of fibers deep in the tree, next the more brittle cracking of branches in the way, then the thud of the trunk striking against the earth. No one spoke for a minute. The tree lay across the path to the

172

orchard like another low wall. Harp and Ellie tried running along its length.

"I'm thankful they're through without any accident. I wouldn't admit it to Josh, but I'm always frightened to death when he decides to cut down a tree," Lucy said.

"But you can see so far now," Phyllis said. "You know, the first day we came I thought it was the most wonderful view . . . of course, I still think so, but I mean it seemed so amazing to have in your own yard."

The beginning and end of summer came together almost too tightly. And "yard." Lucy had a swift image of cramped square-fenced plots in a city neighborhood, and thought again with pity of Phyllis having to leave here tomorrow.

"I thought we'd have supper a little early tonight, Phyl, so we can have one more good long evening by the fire." That was all that was left. Maybe tonight she would have a chance to talk to Jim. Josh and Jim must have more to say to each other. There must be something more.

"We're going to try to leave by five, you know. We ought to go to bed early, I'm afraid," Phyllis said.

When Lucy went down for Phyllis, she found her ironing the ruffled curtains of the cottage. She looked flushed and hot.

"Phyllis, they didn't need washing. Why did you go to all that trouble?"

"Oh, the least I could do was to leave the place ready for the next guests. I'm almost through."

"Such a lot of work, though." Lucy wished Phyllis hadn't. They would just close it for the winter, anyway. The windows of the small living room were bare, and the room itself seemed larger, more like a studio. The bright-blue cover of the couch in the corner seemed to dominate the room. If she moved the loom down here . . . She could see how it would be; a room of her own, dry and snug on rainy days, and she could just go out and lock the door. Now, in an instant, she had come down in the morning, with the light filtering through the orchard, and worked on into the afternoon, when the sun would drift across the meadow. She would get rid of most of this furniture . . . that silly lamp with the crooked shade . . . keep it bare, and paint the floor the color of the couch cover. . . . The only sound was the squeak of the ironing board.

"There, I won't hang the curtains up until I come back from swimming," Phyllis said.

"Don't hang them at all. Just put them in the drawer of the dresser, Phyl. I was thinking I might move the loom down here." She broke off. Would Phyllis think they didn't want them here again?

But Phyllis said, "What a fine idea. I wondered why you didn't use it. Surely, you'll never have guests who come and stay the whole summer again."

"I hope you'll come again," Lucy said, but she felt as though the loom were already there, filling the end of the small living room, crowding them out.

Phyllis said, "I'll get into my suit. I won't be a minute."

Lucy sat down to wait for her. Two bags, already packed, stood by the front door; coats were piled on the chair, and already the house was emptying itself of their living. But as she looked around the room, Lucy remembered the rainy night she had come down to tell Phyllis that Josh had gone back up the mountain for Jim. Two nights ago, when Phyllis rushed down here in anger at Josh, did she pace around this room? And Jim . . . "He spends too much of his time sitting down there, brooding," Josh had said. Her eyes followed the line between the boards. It would be a relief to have them gone.

Phyllis came back in her bathing suit. Because she didn't say anything about the house, Lucy found herself saying, "You did find the little house comfortable?" But she sounded to herself like a landlady.

"Oh, very; it's been splendid for us." And Phyllis was a tenant, generous now that she was moving out.

The others weren't ready, so they went ahead. "Isn't Josh ridiculous doing all this at the last moment?" Lucy asked.

"I think they've had a good time at it," Phyllis said.

"It's going to be cold," Lucy said as they walked across the field to the pool. Each sentence seemed to stand alone, not lead on to the next one.

A scattering of yellow alder leaves lay on the brown surface of the pool. "Like a school of goldfish," Phyllis said. "Only they're too still." She slid into the water without waiting, and Lucy, watching her, saw the shock of the cold in the tightening of her face, and the compression of her mouth.

"You're brave! Braver than I am," Lucy said.

Phyllis swam across the pool and clung to the rock on the other side. "It feels good!" she called back, shaking her head to get the water out of her hair.

Lucy dove, as she had learned to dive at Miss Ingalls's, feeling the arrowy spring in her knees and pushing away from the hard edge of rock with her toes. She swam the length of the pool before she turned and came back to Phyllis and held on to the rock beside her.

"Remember the day we lay on this rock?" Lucy asked. But the others arrived before Phyllis could answer, and the stillness of the wood was shattered by their splashes.

"Last man in is a purple-bottomed baboon!" Harp yelled, holding his nose as he jumped.

But slowly the silence of the deep pool in the wood made itself felt, subduing their voices. Lucy and Phyllis climbed up on the rock, and Josh stretched out full length on the high ground. James sat on the edge, dangling his feet.

"I'll never forget the stillness of this place," Phyllis said in a low voice. They watched the reflection of a bird flying high over the pool before anyone spoke.

"I've never quite known what this place meant in my life," Lucy said. "Mystery, I guess."

James said, "It was my Walden Pond. When we talked of coming this summer, I kept thinking of the mountain and this pond. I mean besides you two," he added, and they laughed.

"I asked Lucy to marry me up here, and it was so solemn I was afraid she wouldn't have me," Josh said, seeming suddenly young.

175

Lucy sat still, remembering that time.

"What is it to you, Phyl?" James asked. "You haven't said."

"I'm not sure," she answered slowly. "Something . . . I guess it's a mirror, an ancient copper one, partly covered with verdigris, the kind you see in museums, but you can still catch a shadow of yourself in it."

James leaned over, seeing his own reflection. "I know what you mean," he said.

In the closeness of the moment, Lucy knew suddenly what she wanted to do.

"All right, you kids," Josh called out. "One more dive!"

"Josh," Lucy said, "why don't you and Phyl take the children, and Jim and I'll come in the other car?" She wanted to talk with Jim; she had been waiting all day, and it was good for Phyllis to go with Josh.

"Fine," Josh said. "Phyl, shall we go on?"

Lucy and Jim went on sitting there after the others had left. They could hear the children singing and Josh and Phyllis joining in. Then there was no sound at all.

"Jim, I couldn't let you go without asking you something," Lucy said. "We've had the whole summer, but somehow we haven't really talked together."

Jim smiled. "In a way, I guess that's right, Lucy, and Josh and I have talked too much."

"Jim," she began again, "are you all right? I mean you're not going away angry or hurt or . . . we haven't failed you, I mean."

"Lucy! I don't know any two people in the world but you and Josh who would have . . ."

She brushed his words off impatiently. "Jim, I meant that about failing you. I somehow feel we have. And it's so stupid to let something come between you and Josh." The words had a stilted sound. "It bothers Josh terribly." She waited for him to say that nothing had.

But Jim said, "It bothers me, Lucy."

She felt herself sucked down now into the cold of the pool. "But what is it? Why it's . . . it's absurd even to talk about it."

Jim was still too long. He sat there breaking a small branch into smaller pieces, tossing them into the water. "I guess it's that I wanted too much of Josh. More than anyone should ask of somebody else."

"What did you want?" Her voice was almost fearful in the quiet that was broken only by the small sound of snapping twigs.

"I wanted Josh to listen . . . to understand what I was telling him, but I see now that if he had, it would mean that someone he's always thought of in one way turns out to be quite different. You can't always know people, even yourself. But Josh doesn't believe that."

"You mean he's wrong."

"I mean that Josh sees his world in one way and he's not going to admit other ways of seeing. There's just one set of motivations for him . . . that's the trouble with that book he's writing. For me, at least."

"But. . ." She watched the leaves lying still on the near-stagnant water of the pool. "Remember, Jim, long ago, you said something about Josh that I've never forgotten. You said you had to understand him. That he couldn't accept some things."

"But I've come to see that even he has to if he's ever going to help anyone else. But then, who can understand anyone, Lucy, or really accept him as he is? We shouldn't expect it; either we should straighten out our own difficulties, or ask a psychiatrist to have a try at them, or let the Hound of Heaven overtake us."

She wasn't quite sure how he meant that. Was he sad, or cynical, or just being impersonal? He sounded as though he'd gone beyond thinking of Josh and himself. She wanted to bring him back into a warm sense of Josh's affection.

"Jim, let me tell you something," she began. "When Phyl called that night last spring and told Josh how upset you were . . ." She felt his quick glance and remembered he didn't know Phyl had called, but it didn't matter now. ". . . Josh couldn't wait to have you here. You see, Jim, how much he cares?"

"I do see that, gratefully."

177

"Then . . ."

"I didn't realize how much I was asking of Josh when I came, or . . ." He reached over for another twig and began throwing pieces into the water. ". . . or how it would come to define our own limitations."

Instinctively, her eyes measured the limits of the brown water and the steep wall of rock on one side. She watched the reflection of the branches sinking out of sight in the pool and thought that nobody had ever really measured its depths. Too close to them, a woodpecker drummed against a tree. She shivered.

"Look, Lucy, you're getting cold. Shall we go? All this hasn't anything to do with my affection for you or Josh, you know that."

Their eyes met for a moment. "I should hope not," Lucy murmured, but her glance moved back to the pool. She walked slowly over toward the gate, wanting him to say something more.

"I like to think of Harp and Phyl knowing this pool," he said as he got into the car.

Phyllis was glad the children sang on the way back and she and Josh could join in so they didn't have to talk. She hadn't been alone with Josh since he had told her . . . her mind still flinched at the actual words . . . since the night in the study. If she could talk with him now, casually, it would be easier when they came to leave tomorrow. She had felt differently about him just now at the pool; she had caught a glimpse of him as he must have been in his twenties, waiting for Lucy to say she would marry him. Now it seemed strange that she had said she hated him. He put back his head and let out a shout at the end of "Mac-Namara's Band," and the children yelled with him.

"I know Lucy wanted to talk with Jim," Josh said as the children began to sing again. "I think she feels she can say some things to him that I've been clumsy about."

He knew he had been clumsy then. And cruel . . . did he know that, too? Anger tightened her throat. She would like him to know that she hadn't bothered James with her worries. She hadn't even . . . she had stopped worrying about James, at least in that frantic, frightened way. Why was it, when nothing was really changed?

The jeep swerved over to the side of the narrow road to avoid the bad rut, and, for a moment, she looked through the tangled wilderness that came too close.

But she had given up hoping that James would ever lose his feeling of guilt. She said the word boldly in her mind. She knew now that she had to leave him alone with it. And not try to pretend that it wasn't so. James would take it in his own way.

The jeep swerved back, and the children sang louder. Josh touched her arm, nodding his head to urge her to sing.

"My Bonnie lies over the ocean . . ." she sang with the rest of them. Josh's voice carried them all. She remembered how strong it had sounded over the phone the night she called him. . . .

They would be home in a minute. This would be the time to thank him. "In spite of everything, Josh . . ." she would say. The children jumped off at the gate, but she rode on up to the house.

Josh said, "Phyl, I don't know how much being here has helped Jim. I've done my best, but I can't seem to get to him. I'm so sorry for him, at the same time that I'd like to shake some sense into him . . . I'm sorry for you, too, Phyllis. If I . . ." Something in his tone of voice or the note of pity stung her mind so she didn't wait to hear the rest of his sentence.

"Thank you," she mumbled, getting out of the jeep.

When she opened the door of the guesthouse, she felt herself pushing past the loom in the room that was already Lucy's studio. She picked up the curtains she had left so carefully spread out on the bed and piled them into the empty drawer of the dresser.

Then she saw her face in the mirror, blotched with red, her mouth tight, her eyes staring back at her. "Pride," she said aloud. "That's what's the matter with you."

Why couldn't she have sat there and talked with Josh instead of going off again, hugging her hurt pride to her?

She pulled open the drawer and straightened the curtains. She had called Josh in the beginning. He and Lucy hadn't promised they could help; they had only wanted to. And she couldn't take what they had given, even the pity, without feeling humiliated.

She peeled off her bathing suit, which was dry now, and walked naked over to the closet to get her clothes.

Twenty-two

W H E N   S H E   W A S   F I N A L L Y in the car, Phyllis leaned on the edge of the door to say again to Lucy, "You were wonderful to make breakfast for us at this early hour." They had eaten under the yellow lamp in the kitchen, just as they had the morning Josh and James went to see Mr. Hopkins, but if the others thought of it, too, they didn't speak of it. Lucy's getting breakfast at five-thirty, Phyllis thought, was just one more kindness she and James had accepted. "There's no use trying to thank you for all you and Josh have done." She had said that before, too, in almost the same words.

And Lucy said again, "We loved having you here."

Lucy seemed a little remote this morning under her warmth. She wished Lucy could have known her better, that she was more like Lucy.

"I wish you didn't have to go just yet," Lucy repeated. "The guesthouse will look awfully lonely. And now that Josh cut that tree down, I'll see it every day and miss you."

"It was such a haven," Phyllis offered. "I'll like to think of you weaving down there."

Then Rich came up to her side of the car. "Maybe I'll get out your way this fall, Phyllis."

"We'll be glad to see you, Rich. We'll show you Chicago." The word "Chicago" sounded strange for a minute. Phyllis glanced at Josh standing by James's side of the car. What could they say now? It was useless to drag out the good-bys. Why didn't James start? He hated to go, after all.

"Ellie couldn't stand your leaving, I think," Lucy said. "She's disappeared."

"She's a darling. I'm going to miss her." Phyllis remem-

181

bered back to Ellie's birthday wish. "We certainly have stayed all summer. Ellie got her wish," Phyllis said. Did it sound wry?

"Well, good-by, Jim," Josh said. "Let me hear from you. Let me know how it goes. Don't wait so long to come again."

"Thanks again, Josh . . ."

Josh came around the car and stopped to say good-by to Harp in the back seat. "We're going to see a lot of you when you come East to school, young man. We hope you'll spend your vacations here the way your father did."

Phyllis felt as she used to in school when the teacher stopped at the desk next to hers. It would be her turn next.

"Good-by, Phyl."

"Good-by, Josh." Everything that had happened, everything they had said tied in a knot in her mind. She felt her eyes wet.

"Thank you, Josh," she managed. But that was what she had said before in the study when she hadn't meant it at all. What good was it to say it now, when she meant it.

Josh said, "I'll always remember you in the Garden of Eden that first morning."

"You mean as a shameless hussy," she retorted. But she thought how different it had been then. What a pity . . . If they had the summer to do over . . .

"Harp!" Ellie came running from the shed, holding out in front of her the boat Harp had built, resplendent in a coat of red paint. "You almost forgot it."

"I don't want it," Harp said.

"Oh, Harp, after Ellie brought it for you," Phyllis said.

"There's nothing wrong about that boat, Harp," Lucy told him.

"O.K." Harp grinned quickly at Lucy.

Ellie threw her arms around James and hid her face against his jacket. "You'll come back next summer, Uncle Jim, won't you?"

"Not next summer, Ellie. Sometime," he promised. "Well, I guess we've got to go. Good-by, Lucy. Thank you again. Good-by, Josh."

The car was moving. Lucy stood with her arm in Josh's.

Ellie was crying against Lucy. Rich waved as he walked off toward the barn.

"Good-by," Phyllis called again, not quite seeing them as the car rolled down the steep hill to the highway.

Lucy and Josh watched the car disappear around the curve in the drive. "We got them off to a good start," Lucy said.

"They'll have a cool day for driving," Josh said, looking up at the sky, which was still gray. The mountain was hidden in the mist, and the newly felled tree and the meadow were covered with moisture. "It very nearly did frost last night," he added.

Lucy shivered. "I got cold out here saying good-by. Come on in, Ellie."

Rich drove up from the barn, but he left his car in the driveway and followed them into the kitchen. "I forgot what time it was. It's too early even to go for the milk," he said, and he spread marmalade heavily on a piece of toast still on the table.

The table under the light was just as they had left it. Lucy looked with distaste at the dishes and the empty chairs and the paper napkins crumpled at each place. It was always depressing when you got people off early. She put the coffeepot on to heat and remembered Phyllis yesterday saying the coffee was sun-warmed.

"Ellie, why don't you go back to bed for an hour or so," she suggested. She wished they all could until this mood was over. Josh stood looking out the window without saying a word.

Ellie shook her head. "Mother, I just thought of something. You forgot to pay us. You forgot to pay Harp."

What was she talking about? Then Lucy remembered. "Oh, I guess I did," she said. "Josh, give Ellie a quarter, please. I'll have to send Harp his."

Josh put his hand in his pocket. "What's this for, Puss?"

"Harp and I took down Raccy's cage and cleaned it all out."

"I thought it was too bad to leave it there and remind

Jim of it," Lucy explained. Sometimes Ellie was so perceptive, and other times she seemed to have no sense at all.

"Jim was still so obsessed with that boy's suicide, I don't know whether he was really any better when he left or not," Josh said.

"Oh, Josh, he was much better. Even Ellie noticed it, didn't you, dear?"

Ellie was kneeling on a chair by the table, pouring salt out of the cellar into an eggshell, but Lucy refrained from telling her not to. "After he let Raccy go, he felt better," Ellie said. Lucy marveled at her deep-blue eyes, so clear that no one could doubt the truth of what she said.

"As a matter of fact," Rich said, still chewing the last piece of his toast, "Jim didn't let the raccoon out."

They waited. Then Josh asked, "Well, who did?"

"I did," Rich said. "I caught him, so I figured I had a right to let him go. I got sick of all the rumpus over how I should take care of him, and all that." A truculent note pitched Rich's voice higher than usual. "I might as well have been in the cage myself."

Although she went on watching Ellie, Lucy felt Josh looking at Rich, Rich looking back at Josh. When she did look at Rich, she thought with irritation that he was enjoying the shock he had given them.

"Did Jim know you let him out?" Josh's voice was low, but it was cold.

Rich shrugged. "I don't know. I guess he had a pretty good idea, and I guess he'd understand why I did it, too."

"It seems all too clear why you did it," Josh said. His voice was edged, but Lucy could see the look of hurt in his eyes. How could Rich do a thing like that!

"I'm sorry I didn't say something before." Rich's tone was still defiant. "But no one ever really asked. You just decided it was Jim."

Nobody spoke, and Rich went on, "You can see how it was. I didn't say anything that night, and then everyone stopped talking about it as though it couldn't be mentioned, so I . . . I let it go."

Yes, Lucy thought, she could understand how it was.

184

Josh must see how it had happened, and Rich could have gone on keeping it to himself. She wished he hadn't sprung it this morning.

"I see," Josh said.

Rich flushed. "Look, I'm going to take the back road and try to catch up with Jim so I can give them a send-off. Anyway, I want to tell him about Raccy. I'll be right back."

Rich rushed out of the kitchen, and they heard his car as he drove off. Lucy had kept Ellie from running after him by a warning shake of her head. Josh put his chair back in its place at the table and went on into his study.

"Mother," Ellie began.

"Ellie, I'm not going to do the dishes just now, so you can run along."

"All right, but, Mother, what made Uncle Jim feel better if he didn't let Raccy out? Do you think it was getting lost on the mountain?"

"Ellie, I don't know. Maybe. It doesn't matter so long as he did feel better, does it?"

Ellie chewed her cheek. "I wish they hadn't gone away." Then she went forlornly upstairs. Lucy poured two cups of coffee and took them into the study.

"I thought we needed another cup," she said.

"Thanks," Josh mumbled. He stirred his coffee for several seconds. "I thought, of course, that Jim had let the raccoon out, because he felt guilty about making that boy do what he wouldn't naturally have done, a kind of symbol of freedom. Why didn't he tell me he hadn't, Lucy? I thought it was an indication of his mental state. Instead of that, he had nothing to do with it; it was just a demonstration on Rich's part."

"I'm glad he didn't do it," Lucy said.

"I told Phyllis he did it," Josh admitted grudgingly. "Jim must have thought I was a great one to advise him or anybody else," he added.

"He wouldn't feel that way, Josh. And he was better at the end of the summer. He'd worked things out so he . . . he understood himself better."

Josh's chair squeaked as he leaned back in it. "I doubt

185

it. He'll just settle down to living with his obsession. He'll never get out of there now; just go on in a kind of dogtrot existence that doesn't begin to require all his capacities."

Lucy recognized the phrase from one of his chapters. There was no point in telling Josh what Jim had said about the book. She drank her coffee, but it had such a flat taste she didn't finish it, and Josh had forgotten to drink his.

"You know, Lucy," he burst out, "I couldn't live with something like that on my mind; feeling responsible for that boy, I mean."

Lucy was silent. Then she said, "It would be hard."

She picked up their cups. "Well, they've gone. It will be good to be alone again."

"Yes," Josh said slowly, "but I think the world of Jim. There isn't anything I wouldn't do for him. Phyllis, too."

"I know," Lucy said, and then she added, "Oh, I know that, Josh. You did everything you could for them."